I0580656

Off A Light

Cover art by Douglas C. Granum.

Cover design by Scott Norris

Copyright © Douglas C. Granum.

All rights reserved. No part of this book may be used or repro-
duced in any manner whatsoever without written permission
except in the case of brief quotations embodied in crtical articles
and reviews.

douglasgranum.com | monkeyhouse-media.com

ISBN 978-1-939723-21-5

First Edition

DOUGLAS C. GRANUM

Off A Light

He did nothing, he didn't deserve to die. Some people said he wasn't dead, some said I was just sleeping somewhere.

And Bill? Some said it was the fourth of July earthquake that rattled, then snapped him. Others said it was Bill's Indian girlfriend. Bill had cuffed the girl for often getting drunk and stoned and making out and sleeping with anyone who wanted her.

Her father, Two Dogs Running, trapped Bill in a small coffee shop down at the Four

Corners, and even though Bill fought his hardest, he was no match for the big Indian.

Her father pretty much destroyed the coffee shop as well as Bill in the process, leaving him nearly dead, bleeding profusely from his right ear, in a coma. Two Dogs Running stood over the collapsed form of Bill and shouted into his bloodied comatose face, while the terrified and panicked coffee barista hid in the small crowded store room a thin door away from Two Dog's rage. He told Bill if he ever came near his daughter Luna again he would kill him, awake or in his sleep. Touch her and he was a walking dead man. They took Bill away in an ambulance with flashing red lights. I saw it all. I was, after all, just sleeping.

Weeks later Bill walked along the shores of the Yoko reservoir. I, his small white Bichon Frisé, Frankie, proudly lead the way on a moss covered slippery trail by the water. Bill saw the mirror like stillness of the

Yoko's surface. Stopping for a moment, he leaned out over the still clear water holding a branch, peered into the mirrored surface, and saw his own haggard face. It was a face he hadn't looked carefully at in a long, long time.

Beneath the water's still tranquil surface, reflected through his face, swam groups of small, dark jade-colored fish grazing on small plants and grubs along the muddy bottom.

Bill, exhausted Bill, depressed Bill, sad, very sad Bill, sat down heavily on an old mossy log with his arm around me, looking out over the Yoko. Darkness, very sad darkness, filled the young man's soul. Bill's thoughts went round and round his brain, a tempest. No up, no down, no joy, no success, no direction, no home, just misery, pure cold unending.

His powerful left arm and hand were around me, holding me close, while in his right hand he held his well-used but still prized 38 Smith and Wesson chromed pistol.

Bill looked down at my small white face, then in a totally unexpected move, roughly pushed me off the log. Then in a burst of despair with an anguished moan, he lifted his pistol, drawing a shaky bead between my loving brown eyes. I looked up at Bill inquisititively, lovingly, trustingly.

Remembering his face, that gaunt reflection, Bill wondered how this moment arrived, how it began, how he ended up looking and feeling this haggard, this useless, this hopeless. Why, where, how did the endless fear in his guts fill his every present waking moment? Was there anything else in this world but gut aches and encompassing fear? Was he ever really happy?

Climbing back up on the old log by Bill, by the water's edge, I lifted my little black nose toward a light breeze wafting from the dark forest behind Bill and me. There was a putrid smell, the death rot of a dead deer laying off in the woods somewhere, killed most likely by the frozen winter. I could smell spring, I could smell the curly wild rose, I could smell the unhappiness on Bill's breath, watching as he took another drink from the bottle of amber liquid he constantly held.

Bill's breath was sad and thick. From time to time he thumbed the double action hammer of his prized chromed 38 Smith and Wesson, rolling over the chambers filled with copper jackets, death in each hollow point, then slowly letting the hammer silently fall without firing.

Thinking back he remembered he was happy once, long ago. He was a little blue-eyed cherubic golden blond. He was maybe four or five years old. There was the water. The beach was steep with loose black discs of smooth rock. They were glossy and slid on each other. He threw some of them into the water while Paddington, his dog at the time, ran into the water after them.

He remembered he was playing with a small wooden boat old Grandpa Levenseller had made for him. The paint on the little boat was still damp in places. Some of it came off on his hands and thighs where he held the little red boat. On both sides of the bow of the little red boat old Grandpa Levenseller had written, "Bill". Grandpa chuckled in his soft way when he handed Bill the boat that he had made.

His mother and father sat on a silver-grey drift log partly hidden in tall blue-green grass. It was windy, he remembered the bending of the tall blue grass to the wind. He remembered the cigarette smoke from his parents cigarettes drifting, filtering up from the grasses. He also remembered clouds, drifting and dark. Patches of shadows on the water filtered across the distant inlet.

He was young, yet he still remembered everything except his near death.

He watched his parents engage in events of gluttony that seemed to leave them winded. He watched his mother tipping French fries from her greasy lips down her mouth, grotesquely grinning at his father. She washed the French fries down with Russian Stolichnaya vodka straight from the bottle. She wiped her grease glistening lips with her tongue, took a long, slow, deep drag on her Lucky, coughed deeply, then squinted her eyes at the smoke. She reached for a chicken wing and handed the vodka to Bill's father. He grabbed the bottle while flipping his cigarette far out into the tall lush blue-green grasses.

Bill remembered a dog, a small white and black short haired terrier that tried to bite him. His dad had gotten very mad and kicked the dog, which ran off yelping to an old woman. The dog's owner, the old woman, was sitting in a black and chrome wheel chair where her family had parked her, then left.

The old woman shook her umbrella at Bill's dad. She wanted water and the dog more or less barked constantly while showing his teeth.

Bill's dad went back to our little camp and poured some vodka and soda water in a paper cup with some ice and gave the old woman half of a chicken sandwich. He gave the little black and white dog some pieces of chicken. The old woman thanked Bill's dad and the dog licked his dad's hand.

Bill, then called Billy, was young, however he remembered it all this day while sitting on that old log by the Yoko, since that day he nearly drowned. He didn't know he had almost died, since he didn't die. There were many surprises to come in his young life. This was also just about the time the beatings from his mother began.

First when she was drinking, and even when she was sober, she started to viciously threaten little blond, blue-eyed Billy. Next she threw things at him when his father was at work and she was drunk. She sat mostly with her skinny yellow legs apart at the kitchen table, smoking, drinking, laughing, cackling. Sometimes she spat at Billy.

She and Bill's father had no relationship except smash-mouth brutal kinds of sex, drinking, and barely disguised hatred for each other, little blond Billy, and their sad desperate world around them. Respect for each other was not a word they knew. His mother's sexual needs were desperate, but love was not involved.

Somehow in this madness they laughed, though only when polluted and drunk. Then when plastered, they engaged themselves in events of gorging where they would stuff and cram food, then go out in

the yard lean a hand against the log truck
and puke it all up. Then back to the bottle to
wash away the taste of sour vomit.

"Grab me a chicken wing!" she would
shout at Bill's dad through a drunken haze.

They circled the filthy little kitchen,
drunk, crawling on the floor, harangu-
ing one another. They eyed distant moldy
plates of cookies, pieces of cake with rock
hard frosting, cold beef that when turned
over at times was covered with maggots.
They courted these plates of food like distant ritual objects of sacred value.

Their desires were not ignored, they ate
whatever and whenever they wanted. They
gnashed and ground the food with rotten
molars, masticating. They chewed little Billy's food and handed it to him out of their
mouths. Billy remembered the food from
their drunken mouths tasted like rancid
grease, cigarettes, and vodka, always vodka.

They courted each other by rubbing

their stomachs and mouths, osculating like licking, fucking dogs. Though from time to time there were sensual words, the real topic was food. Though they talked sex, which never happened, only copious amounts of food happened.

Little blond, cherubic, blue-eyed Billy was a happy baby in a deeply unhappy family. His cooing and giggling baby language became unusual. He wasn't taught words like love, kitty, puppy, Mama loves you, goo goo, Da-Da. He had no Nana. Nope, no words like that.

Billy didn't have a sweet, comfortable, warm, cozy place in that desolate little house. Billy was a nomad in his own house. His parents kept no normal, ordinary hours. Some nights his father would bring home hamburgers, pickled pigs feet, barbecue ribs, a panoply of cheap foods of all kinds at midnight after drinking all evening at the Golden Horseshoe bar.

Conversation wasn't around the table, since the table hadn't been cleared in months. Sometimes Billy stood on a chair and washed the dishes while his mother quietly drank and smoked Lucky Strikes, no filter. His mother acerbically told him he would never amount to more than a pile of shit and be a dishwasher for the rest of his mean, miserable life. He giggled, not knowing what she meant.

His home life was isolated, mostly since his mother and father ignored him in favor of the Stoly bottle. He was an only child growing surprisingly strong in very poor and sad soil.

Often times they gave little Billy vodka off of the tips of their cigarette stained fingers to help him sleep, winking at each other. Sometimes they poured vodka into his Coke in a glass with ice and laughed uproariously when he got drunk.

They cursed him when he threw it all

up on the floor, punishing him by making him clean up his own vomit and putting him to bed without dinner.

He was an only child. How innocent is a child? How vulnerable was Billy? This little person, this precious little blond cherub, an adorable photograph today, a deeply troubled adult next? What happens what can happen to abused damaged children, read on.

His mother was skinny with parchment hard, yellowing, tobacco stained skin. Her skin was the same color as the tobacco, nicotine stained walls.

Billy by startling contrast, was soft, pink, sweet, loving.

Billy had few toys he played with. Sometimes he had crumpled cigarette packages, cigar boxes, old engine parts, and a gorilla doll named Ivan that Billy's dad won from a punch board at the Golden Horseshoe.

Billy slept in his dad's oily, dirt encrust-

stone drunk husband as he crawled around the floor trying to get away from her lethal blows. Some nights Billy's father took little Billy and Paddington and slept in his log truck parked out on what was once a lawn, now a muddy rutted mess, with smashed beer cans and further out in the yard empty whiskey bottles, everywhere cigarette butts, like a yellow snow storm.

Thinking now Bill remembered sticks of dynamite on the littered table in their dilapidated house on the edge of the forest. No one ever visited. The dynamite lay in a bed of waxed butcher paper.

The wax paper was the color of the belly of a dead fish he remembered on the graveled beach. Some nights his father, drunk, raging while screaming and coughing, lit stick after stick of the red dynamite and threw them out into the Yoko.

Dead fish were floating on the surface in the early morning sunlight. The booming sounds echoed up through the mountains, finally being swallowed up by the endless stands of enormous quiet redwoods. Owls flew.

His father drove log trucks. He was good at it. He was also a rigger and a topper, very dangerous jobs, he was good at both. His men liked him, his wife loathed him, his infant son and his dog, Paddington, idolized him and were his only true friends.

Working all day falling gigantic redwoods on steep rocky mountain slopes had its way with him, nearly fatalistic. He climbed trees growing off hanging rock faces to trim them limb by monstrous limb down to the ground. Then he would climb back to their far top with climbing spurs and axel grease the whole tree to the bottom. Then at the bottom once more, he'd crank his razor sharp Stihl chainsaw with its six foot blade, then with expert precision, notch the tree leaving enough of a hinge to pull it just so, just where he wanted to drop it.

He aimed it so that it was felled straight and true down the mountain side, sliding and ending up floating in the Yoko.

He could do this. His wife, his drunken, bitchy wife, hag that she was, hated him for every good thing he did or could do. At the end of it she lived a life of darkness. Hate was her master, heavy drinking her fuel, masturbation and child abuse her constant.

Years ago as a young up and coming logger Billy's father bought a new Mack truck. He bought it before he was married. He had plans, big plans. Before he got married he thought, pursued, dreamed he would go down to the flat lands, go to college. He knew just how he was going to do it. He had graduated top in his little high school, and he had to make a five year plan before he could graduate. His counselor saw in him all the promise that he himself felt. In those early days he had that wonderful attribute called attitude.

That was now a distant memory. Neither his counselor nor himself could have imagined the train wreck that was fast approaching when a slender, dark-haired beauty first spotted him. She was light tan in color, had flashing eyes, long blue-black hair, Irish and French Canadian. If, as has been said, all beauty has some imperfection, hers was her slack mouth. Large luscious lips, but something was just a click off.

When he first met her she drank coffee, black as axel grease, thick as mud, with cardamom, small cups filled with grounds, several shots at a time. Even then, a warier individual would have spotted her predilection, her addictive qualities. Her personal beauty was wasted on her, it meant nothing to her. She ruined herself and savaged those around her.

She chain smoked, the sink filled with

burnt butts leaving small yellow riverine stains on the bottom of the sink where the cigarettes had burnt themselves out, little flat tuna-fish cans over flowing with cigarette butts littered the kitchen table, living room table, the night stand beside their bed, the top of the TV cabinet, the lawn outside the front door, all was layered with butts. She coughed constantly, a sickly, rattling, greenish-yellow sputum filled wet sound.

Billy's dad came home most nights after dark from the Golden Horseshoe bar where he ate pickled pigs knuckles, smoked Lucky Strikes, and drank Jack Daniel's whiskey.

First a chew of the pig, then toss back a shot of jack followed with a nod to the bartender for one more, a ritual the bartender knew, then a deep, chest searing, tearing drag on his Lucky Strike, then turned his head with the back his hand over his mouth and give a loud cough at the sawdust covered floor at the foot of his bar stool. Then it was all repeated again. Shake out another Lucky from his worn, green-black checked logger's shirt, cup his hand around the wooden lit match around the end of the Lucky take another drag, nod at the bar tender, a double this time, then flush the whiskey between his meerschaum tobacco stained teeth.

Sitting at the corner bar stool, where he always sat, he thought how useless his life was and what a failure he was. He hated his life and his wife. Sometimes he thought about Billy, but mostly he sat darkly hunched over a drink and smoked, then coughed.

Over and over mold encrusted, tessellated, endless sewer pipes of the same thought. Sanity exists in the small ritual, and this small ritual didn't work any longer for Billy's dad. Desperation reined, his sanity was dissipating.

He knew he could never be drunk

enough to face his wife, even if he passed out. When he awoke from his drunkenness, she would still be there. This grotesque leering nightmare, that at some distant time he had loved.

He shook his head love is strange, he thought. He was smart, he knew this yet somehow he was in a morass.

His reality was distorted he could, but only now when he was drunk remember his realities. He remembered that his reality depended on how he saw things:

warmth, love, joy, caring, sweetness, holding, sharing, attending, feeling, freely kissing, hugging, smiling, sharing, dancing, endless fields of of wild flowers in the high Sierra's, trembling spirit of young love, he knew he couldn't always get what he wanted but there was a time when he dreamed he could, he knew he could, now he was frighted all of the time and it stopped him stone cold. He fumbled in his shirt pocket for the Lucky pack, while at the same time nodding to the bar tender.

What he was doing tonight he had done many times before, so so many times, and it always ended the same way. Percentages had swung out of his favor. He saw no lightness, only dark.

When he got exhausted at the pool table and bored at darts and out of small change for the punch boards he wearily pulled himself off of the bar stool, stumbled out into the dark, a stuffed toy won at the dart board tucked beneath his arm, to where his large dirty old Mac truck idled out back of the bar, shooting black diesel into the pure mountain air.

He had drank until he felt he could still manage to drive his huge rig through the mountainous roads, navigate the graveled rutted curves, yet still drunk enough to face his scrawling, scratchy wife.

"Oh God," he would moan over the dim

lights of the dashboard. "How I hate her, how I hate her. Oh God, what has happened to my once fresh life?" There is nothing, he thought, worth this constant wear, there is no winning only losing, each alcohol sodden day, gulp by gulp. Someday, I will die, and what will become of Billie, what a miserable son of a bitch I have become, what a piss poor father.

He parked his mud drenched logging truck on what was left of his lawn, climbed down into the mud, flipped his cigarette into the dark, headed for the dark door of the house.

She met him at that same door every night, drunk, bitchy, unless she was passed out watching sit-coms on T.V.

She could hear him coming from miles away along the mirror calm silent fragrant mountain roads along the Yoko. Taking two shots of Stoly in quick succession, she threw the shot glass into the sink filled with cigarette butts, breakfast plates, lunch plates and plates from who knew when, they were always moldy.

She drunkenly crouched, evilly chuckling, a type of ambush, then ripped open the door when she heard his foot falls on the porch.

The damp stale smells from the house told the tale. It was first vodka, then sour, heavy cigarette breath, then burnt baby food, then more stale cigarettes, then who knew, dirt.

She was mean and meant to hurt him. There was nothing kind in her world, only biased, polluted anger.

The first words Billy learned as a baby were screeched in heat and fury at his father from his always strung out mother.

"Get the hell out! Leave you son of a bitch, I don't need you. Bastard, I will kill you in your sleep, die, so I can find some peace."

These and other words became Billy's early vocabulary.

The words were jarring, harsh.

"Fuck, fuck, fuck, I detest your guts." His mother continually hammered away, screeching in his father's drunk, exhausted, sad face.

Billy's first sentence, proudly spoken in front of his father was, "Shit hook." He didn't know what it meant, he thought it sounded funny.

He was taken into his parents bedroom with the worn tan linoleum floor, had his pants pulled down, and was severely spanked by his drunken, polluted mother.

When she stopped her beating, she passionately, drunkenly, slobberingly kissed him. His face was covered with his own tears, her jet black mascara, her spit and her tears.

His family had a dog then, he remembered Paddington his whole life. Paddington was a large golden Saluki-Russian wolf hound his father had found in an animal shelter. Perhaps he had saved young Billy's life, for when ever the beatings started, he gave an ominous warning, deep in his venous throat with his lips pulled back, exposing his large curved ripping teeth, while making a thunderous threatening sound.

The trip to the beach began in their dirty old blue Ford four door. Billy sat alone in the back seat, looking out the open window smiling while humming to himself, Paddington by his side, ears flying, beard ripped back by the wind. It was a happy looking scene, if you were in a passing car, but inside the little blue Ford desperation reigned.

Thinking back all those years now, Bill remembered thinking it was a long drive. Remembered, but why had he remembered? He was way too young to remember, but he did, even from this long vantage of his history. What happened that day? Then he remembered this very important moment somewhere in his life.

Bill thought, "Do I remember it? Did I dream it? Did it happen?"

Dreams and reality are so close. Does it really matter all these many years later if it was a dream or if it really happened?

Sitting on the old mossy log by the water's edge, Bill mused, his elbow on his knee, his head bowed, his hand on his cheek.

Then, like a dark cloud passing over his thoughts, with a cold shiver, he began thinking back again to that day at the beach so long ago. As he thought back, he remembered there was the icy water, he was really quite young, maybe four or five years old.

Bill was young then but he remembered it all, for on that day, he now remembered, he nearly died. He didn't know he almost died since he didn't die, he was too young to remember, but his dad told him the story.

There were many surprises to come in his young life, this was also just about the time the beatings began. He is starting to piece his younger self together.

Paddington, on that day golden as the sunset, lay up in the grasses watching Billy run into the icy cold water, then jump up laughing, his chubby pink angelic body light red from the fridged water, then run up the beach again, his small round body covered with pearls of water glistening in the clear mountain sunlight. Billy would stand there for a moment, looking quizzically at his mother and dad who were groping, kissing, smoking, and drinking.

Then squealing his loudest, looking at his mom and dad again, they didn't see him, he ran headlong down, plunging into the arctic water. Paddington watched this procedure with worry, growling low, deep rumbling sounds in protest.

Somehow Billy was having so much

fun he was running into the water falling down, then getting up again and running back up the black rocky shingled beach.

He ran in again, fell, and jumped up proudly, looking at his mother and father. They didn't see him looking. He needed them to look, he wanted them to see him. He was so proud of himself. Look, look at me. They didn't know he was alive.

He wanted them to see how fast he could run, how brave he was plunging into the icy water. They were gulping Stoly vodka straight out of the bottle.

Looking adoringly, quizzically at them again, Billy turned, laughing, squealing, running back down the black gravel beach, and threw himself into the polar water. The invigorating water, the freezing lake, the killing lake, then he couldn't breathe.

He was beneath the surface of the windy surface of the water. He could see the murky water, he could see the bottom, he was laughing, he was dying.

"Piss on it all, I'm the one dying here," his mother was yelling while he was drowning. "None of this I signed up for, you hear me? I'm isolated in this two bit place, you bastard. And the kid, I don't want the kid. Remember the brat was your idea."

His mother's angry voice screeched above the light soughing breeze. "You made me do this. What an asshole. Speaking of the kid, where is he, I thought he was swimming or something? Where's the kid?"

Billy was drowning, expiring, he could not breathe.

Then, through the blue-green water he saw his father's shoes and pants running, kicking up the muddy lake bottom. Through the sunlit water, the murky water, next to his father's legs were the feathery dog paddling feet and legs of Paddington.

He felt his father's strong logger's hands grab him beneath his arms and lift him up in a great liquid swoosh into the clear invigorating clear mountain air.

His father cried, "Oh Jesus Christ, my son, my son, my precious son," holding him so close.

Billy was laughing and coughing, while his father was crying copious tears. Paddington pranced and howled and talked.

His mother was shouting from where she had stumbled and fallen into the drift wood.

"What a fuck head, why the fuck did you let him do that for?" she drunkenly slurred. "He could have drowned, not that that would have been so bad." Billy's dad backhanded her for that.

"Softly and tenderly Jesus is calling, calling oh sinner come home," the radio purred in the car on the road going home.

It started to heavily rain, the wind shield wipers pushing aside water. Billy started to cry, his mother in the distant front seat was laughing and drinking straight shots from the same Stoly bottle. His dad was quiet and stared down the twisting road, saying nothing. Once in a while he saw double and triple, it was the vodka, yet he never closed his eyes. He was a log truck driver, they didn't crash.

Paddington lay wet and secure beside Billy on the seat, watching and listening. He has his feathered feet and honey brown legs across the white thin legs of Billy, who was whimpering piteously, his wet pants a sopping mound on the car floor.

The real beatings had begun when Billy wet his pants at grade school. The teacher, Miss Jones, made him stand up and face front to the whole class with the large dark pee spot clearly evident on his little jeans. Through a torn hole in his jeans his bony knee could be seen.

The teacher called Billy's mother who, enraged and crazed, barged into the classroom without knocking, and jerked Billy meanly from the room.

"What are you little bastards looking at?" she shouted at the students, her breath was sick and disturbed, she had been drinking. She smelled heavily of cigarettes. She spit at the teacher.

The teacher closed the door, and called the principle. After Billy and his mother left, the room continued to smell of cigarettes and alcohol. The teacher took the students to the gym to let the stench clear from their home room.

When she got Billy into the little blue Ford, she stripped him, pulled off his wet, pee soaked pants and strapped him into the back seat, roughly. He started to cry again, bare, cold, and afraid. His mother berated him all the way home. How can you piss your pants you little nit wit, maybe back to diapers for you, she laughed, diapers huh, huh?

When they arrived home, she pulled him from the car, smothered him in kisses, and carried him into the house to her bedroom. Her bedroom smelled like powdered roses.

His mother dropped him roughly onto the pink silk sheets of her bed and pulled off his blue and white striped T-shirt. He lay there naked, afraid, whimpering while watching as she took the rubber band out of her long stringy black hair. Her greasy hair fell around her shoulders like a bat's wing.

Next she went to her closet and took out a red silk blouse hanging on a steel coat hanger. She took off her shirt and bra, her breasts erect and excited, then put on the red silk blouse, no bra.

She then grabbed the steel coat hanger and pulled it into the shape of a leather strap. She grabbed the Stoly bottle on the night stand, taking a long drink, and took a puff from a cigarette, carefully putting it in the ash tray.

Billy only remembered the first sharp cutting blow, he bled in pain on the pink sheets. Bleeding on the sheets infuriated his mother. She hit him harder. Paddington stood on his hind legs outside at the bedroom window, deeply growling, barking and piteously whining at his inability to stop the beating.

Finally his mother stopped hitting him, winked at him, he remembered the running mascara, her small pointed breast hanging partly out of her red blouse, her nipple erect and florid, the cloying smell of roses, then she leaned over him and passionately kissed him while fervently licking his salty blubbering bleeding lips.

Back on the Yoko.

I looked up at Bill Kriedler as he suddenly stood up from the mossy log as though he had made up his mind about something. The wind had ceased, a cloud covering the sun. The smell of the dead deer was stronger on the damp air of approaching rain. Everything was stilled in anticipation of what?

Then in a sweeping gesture Bill reached down, moaning, "Oh God damn it."

He grabbed me and threw me as far as he could out into the lake. At the same time he reached for his 38 Smith and Wesson, leveled it on me, frantically swimming, my small white head just visible out in the grey shadowed lake. Bill Kriedler brought the 38 to bear on my small white head, then jerked the trigger. At the next and same moment he turned the still smoking muzzle of the highly lethal 38 to his own soft sweating temple, and once more jerked the trigger.

The roar was deafening, Bill Kriedler's world went dark. Time became non existent.

Bill Kriedler was dreaming. He was dreaming he was seven years old again. He was dreaming his mother was kissing him.

His head hurt where she had just hit him with a large wooden butter ladle on the side of his temple. She was kissing him, her tears running down over his face. She usually cried when she beat him. He pried open his eyes, is world was blurry, what he could see was red, his scalp was on fire with pain. He was lying on his back on the other side of the old green moss covered log.

Frankie was licking Bill's face, his lips, his cheeks. As he did, water dripped on Bill's heated face from Frankie's soaking fur.

Bill was in shock, shaking uncontrollably. His scalp was bleeding profusely. He passed out again. Frankie forever and always Bill's friend, stayed close by his side.

I watched ducks quietly slowly swimming on the lake, watched ravens glide over and around me, looking down. Higher in the blue, vultures swept the air while their black shadows brushed over Bill and me.

Finally, watching Bill for a while longer, sitting, whining, licking Bill's wound, I finally curled up close beside him as the last rays of sun went dim, then out. It was cool, and grew from twilight to dark in the mountainous eastern Sierras. The air was fresh.

From somewhere in the steep redwood covered mountains behind us there was the sounds of wolves howling. I stirred, sat up, and moved even closer to Bill.

In the gloomy obscurity of the near surrounding woods there were small packs of coyotes yipping and crying. I lifted my small white muzzle to the twilight sky and sobbed out an ancient song with my high Sierra ancestors. The coyotes stopped their yipping and answered my pleas with mournful howls of their own. The dirge was distant and ancient, a wild place where death came on stained ivory fangs.

Bill had lost control in every direction of

his life. A rusty knife that cut him in every direction. He had lost his will to live and his will to die. He was in an infinity, a kaleidoscope of colors, all sickeningly whirling. In his black throbbing coma he muttered and wept. He had forgotten his name. He had forgotten my name and called me Paddington. I looked at Bill in his coma, starring intently. My stomach hurt. The howling of the distant wolves grew closer now as darkness hovered. It was joined by more barks and yips. I growled, pulling back my lips, coughing at the darkening forest.

I could hear the snarling growls as the wolf pack discovered the rotting deer carcass by their primal yelps and maniacal, screaming barks. The putrid smell of rot grew stronger and gagging as the winter kill was ripped open.

It grew darker, then utterly night. There was the punishing sound of snarling and my wildly beating heart. These two sounds

I could hear in quiet moments, and as the moon lit the Yoko, all grew calm and quiet.

Bill remained all night in his coma, thrashing, blubbering, bawling, while at times deathly still. I licked and cleaned Bill's wounds and slept close to him, when I could sleep.

Metallic orange dawn descended on the desperate scene behind the old rotted moss covered log at the Yoko's shore.

Off across a dew laden meadow, the gold colored quaking aspen's leaves gently fluttered and quivered, lightly dancing in the light early dawn airs. The air flow had changed from down the mountains to up the mountain, bringing with it a sweet and gentle fragrance arising off the surface of the Yoko, and with this purifying breeze, the smell of deer rot went away and was replaced by the fresh, sweet fragrance of fresh mountain water. Trout, silver fingers, rose into the dawn airs after insects.

Turning to a quiet rustling sound I saw out of the early morning shadows at the edge of the back lit forest behind Bill and me, that a large white wolf was loping right at us, disappearing in a small depression, then appearing again, and then loped to a stop. The large wolf then walked slowly, inquisitively on stiff, stork-like legs towards us. His hackles were high on his back and his white muzzle was bloody from eating and gnashing the putrid rotting deer.

Stopping, he surveyed the scene in front of him. Me, a snarling small white dog, the faint smell of despair from the human, and maybe the smell of weakness? The wolf liked weakness, it was almost always to his advantage.

The large white Sierra wolf made a slow stalk towards us, his nose twitching. I growled my most ferocious growl, a desperate, teeth bared growl. The wolf snarled and made a sort of feint at me, like he would a rat, then stopped. I made a sort of run at the wolf. The wolf was shocked and surprised.

Nature was soft and beautiful round this dire scene. Clouds drifted over the high Sierras, trout jumped in the lake, the smell of pine and sage became stronger as the morning got warmer. There were butterflies, lots and lots of butterflies.

Does nature recognize life and death? Was the great white wolf only surviving? Was I dreaming, or was I on that endless road to dying? Looking back at Bill lying on his back in a coma, I could smell the bloody furrow the bullet had carved through his scalp. So could the ravenous inquisitive great white.

Bill dreamt of his mother. Jarring was how Bill described it later when he was first hit in the face with the large wooden butter spoon. His mouth was bloody and black with dried blood, his lips were split and grotesque. His mouth was raw and his front tooth was knocked loose.

His mother grabbed him passionately and kissed his black blue distended lips. He remembered that he was eight, there was a birthday cake with eight candles. She kissed him fervently, her tears and mascara covering his face. Then he felt her shaking hand, trembling hand, on his blue and white stripped gingham shorts.

Somewhere in the far forest a raven cried, the sound echoed off the lake and mountains. What tricksters the ravens are, they see and know all.

The great white wolf advanced closer to us. Bill did not stir. I growled my most ferocious growl. The wolf, hackles up, tail straight out continued, slowly but surely moving forward. This wolf was a veteran of many battles. He made his moves cautiously and deliberately. He was the leader of the pack, and his prowess and survival depended on his finely tuned instincts.

Back of the advancing wolf, near the edge of the forest, three more wolves with tawny grey coats slid through the pines and aspens. They crept, they pranced they crawled, they whined, groveled, they lay still for a moment, heads between their outstretched front legs, gradually but steadily advancing through the sage, ultimately stopping close behind their alpha leader, the great white, their tongues lolling out.

I looked at Bill, then at the wolves. The white made a sort of leap forward where upon I, baring my teeth, maniacally ran at the wolf. The wolf did not move. It pulled back its pink lips, baring its yellow stained teeth.

How did I get the energy, the courage, to summon up the outrageous strength, the mad impossible challenge, the shear guts to run at certain death?

It was love. Love is like this. I would give my life saving Bill Kriedler. Bill Kriedler would take my life, then his own. Why not take his own life and let me live?

Was it Bill's anger? Was it because of the hatred his mother had instilled in him? Misery lived in that sad little house with the small closet of a bedroom, with the window so high you couldn't see out and, more importantly, no one could see in.

Two other wolves, tails wagging high, loped across the sage, yelping and squealing towards me, where I stood facing the great white. I was out of my mind with fear and helplessness. My advantage was my speed for a short distance, but my most valuable advantage was my agility. However, with a wolf pack, none of this made a difference. I belonged to the wolves, and they knew it. All of this didn't matter since I refused to leave Bill lying unconscious beside the rotten log.

The great white, certain that this was a battle he would win, advanced with his plume of a tail wagging ominously back and forth, twitching.

I felt sure death coming my way. The wolves had sifted out of the forest and formed a semi-circle around behind the great white.

I backed up to a snow bank piled high near by the log and lake. Scrambling up its icy side, I stood at the top, coughing and spitting, snarling and screaming really, as the great white terror came to the bottom of the snow bank and, in a way laughing, started up the icy slope, his tail held high.

I bared my teeth, caught between the wolf and the Yoko. I could smell the wolf's dead deer breath as he advanced slowly, surlily, intently up the snowy bank closer to my little black nose.

This was death, white death, ripping gashing tearing death, certain. Oh life, how precious, how unpredictable, how frail I felt at that moment.

At this exact moment a thunderous roar rang out, and the wolf's grinning face dissolved into a great red mangled mass. He twitched not a moment, instead he collapsed instantly and slid down the ice snowy dome into the Yoko, his rich red blood bleeding into the cold clear spring waters. Around his great white head the crimson water was suddenly filled with small fish feeding on the wolf's rich blood. Somewhere among the snowy white high redwoods a raven called. Off deep on the other side of the Yoko came an answer. The wolf pack vanished into the forest.

Bill, with his smoking 38 Smith and Wesson in his hand, sat heavily back down on the rotten moss covered log. I ran, squealing, and jumped into Bill's lap, licking tears from his eyes.

It was raining on the eastern Sierras. Bill was older, he still occasionally bit his fingernails. He was a large handsome muscular blond young man working in the woods with his father.

His passion was to be a writer and get out of logging. His graduating class in high school was thirteen. He was at the top. Yet everyone knew everyone else's private business in that small rural community.

They all remembered little Billy with the pee-soaked pants. There were four girls in his graduating class and none would give him a second look, though in truth, he didn't want their second look.

He worked in the woods as a rigger on the high line. His father, who was lead, berated him and bullied him at every turn. Bill could do nothing right in his father's angry, booze soaked, unhappy life.

Bill was excellent at what he did. He could rig, top, fix diesel engines, in the logging trade he could do it all to a high degree. But at the end of every day he wanted to run, his guts ached. The nearest town was seventy-five miles away. He knew no one there. Bill was alone. He had always been alone. Violent abuse left him isolated. Babies can love, parents can hate. It is rarely the other way around.

Something in his young life had to give. Pressure builds, then bursts. He no longer wished to follow in the footsteps of his father for he knew he must seek a new path of his own and far away from the Yoko.

One day the pressure had finally reached the breaking point. He had to leave his miserable family forever. He realized there wasn't and never would be a future there, neither in his pathetic family or the community, such as it was.

He looked around at his former class mates, rotten teeth, no education, alcoholics, poor health, old before their time. The women of his high school were burdened with too many children, and it was apparent by the way they carried themselves, their young lives were over and they didn't give a damn. Fuck it all, pass the bottle, who's got a Lucky?

Bill's inner voice screamed run.

One day not long after he quietly walked into the shabby, rundown house in his muddy corked logging boots. His mother looked at him aghast, started to shout and berate him pointing to the mud and the floor. He, held out his hand in her face while he grabbed a few belongings, scooped me up, walked past this drunk, cigarette smoking, gaping mother and left, no words necessary. Where he was going he didn't know, but he knew why. He had to to survive or drown in a miasma of depression and despair and end up looking like the rest of the sad, sad community.

Some how he knew that we belong to the power we choose to obey and he chose and knew that what didn't destroy him would make him stronger. He knew here in this little high Sierra logging town there was only weakness.

He never looked back, that part of his life was over. He had no family except me and few belongings except his plum crazy 1971 purple 426 Hemi Cuda convertible which he had purchased some years ago. Fueling up at a small gas station, he threw all of his logging gear into the service station garbage.

"My God," he thought, "how freeing."

Like a butterfly shedding its old skin, he laughed, scooped me up, and shouted into the rain dark, "Let these wings learn to fly! Let's roll, Frankie."

It was dark out on the freeway. I was sitting in Bill's lap, it was 102 degrees in Las Vegas and pouring a deluge of hot desert rain. We drove, splashing through deep puddles of rain, and in the misty headlights a sign, North I-395.

The streets were glossy, wet, oily, slippery. The top was down and the rain went over the top of us on the humid fast wet freeway. Looking into Bill's eyes you would see tears being driven back alongside his cheeks. Look at his mouth and you would see the biggest smile possible.

He pulled me close to him, kissed me on top of my silky head and said, "Frankie, we are going to have a great time, and you know what? It's only the beginning. See that sign, Franks? Highway 395 North. What say we head for Seattle?"

That first night out of Las Vegas we slept in the car behind a little white country church in the parking lot. It's easy to forget, but the Hemi-Cuda has a spacious rear bench seat. I slept on the purple velvet ledge under the rear window. The next day we drove and stopped beside rivers and in fields by barns and ate the rest of yesterday's rations.

Heading north up by Alturas the weather became colder. We decided to stop to warm up. As evening came on we stopped at a little bark-covered log cowboy bar, a county off the northern California line, near Goose Lake.

We pulled into a little parking space between two logging trucks. Their wheels were taller than the Cuda's convertible top. Bill shut off Roy Orbison's "Dream". With the music off I could hear the big rigs were both running.

"What say you, Frankie? Shall we stop?" I held up a paw, so we did, I wish we hadn't.

There were cow trucks, pick-ups, cattle trailers, horse trailers. Occasionally a horse would whinny in the quiet air and kick out at the trailer wall.

"God damn you, Butch. Do that again and I'm going to make you walk, you ole-hammer head," I heard someone with a western twang shout in the dark.

Walking up on the dust worn porch into the bar I noticed it was nearly covered in neon signs. Bill read some: Seven Seas, Coors, Molson, Modelo Negra, Pale Moon, Four Sixes.

"They're all there," said Bill. "Must be a hundred neon signs." He laughed and said, "Must be one hell of an electric bill." We turned to walk into the bar.

I want to say one thing before we enter this smokey, dusty, patron packed local western bar: Everybody knows everybody. In their terminology, "If you ain't from there, they damn well know it, and you're down a click just comin' through that crappy old beat up swinging door."

One other thing about Bill, I don't know what it is, but all of the bitches in heat find him first, and their men, if they are around, don't like him because their women swoon over him. They love him.

Total dog-like, except here they didn't

"I'll take care of ya, just sit with your legs apart."

Then she laughed a hideous smoked cougher's cackle, coughing. Bill sat me down on the split vinyl green chair with shredded yellow grey stuffing pushing out. Her immense shadow landed over me suddenly.

"Well, well, what have we got here?" She patted me with her food smelling hand and gave me a broken doggie bone out of her greasy smelling stained apron.

As Bill sat down I jumped from the ripped vinyl chair to the top of the table by the fogged window. In France, we Chien sit on tables. I am French, you know, raised in France. Raised in a small French village on the coast of Normandy called Honfleur. I often dined on sheep that fed on the Salicornia that grew abundantly, giving the lamb a salty taste on the flats around Mont' Sainte Michael. Here also I ate the most delicious oysters in my life, the magnificent "Cancale" oyster, the brine instilled by the eternal sea.

In France petite, well-formed dogs like me sit on the table tops, very civilized and polished.

There we are part of the event instead of being "ivre mort," or under the table.

Our masters give us snacks off of their plates, waiters offer little crystal bowls of water pour "Le Monsieur Chien." You know France is a place where the populace knows how to eat. We Chien are given magnificent parties at our birthdays, sometimes our pictures featured in Le Paris Match newspaper. We go out to dinner in le haute cuisine restaurants of France. We dress sometimes for the occasion, coats and ties. We are revered and praised, generation to generation with the continuing family. In France we sleep with our masters and mistresses, we dine off of the same Sévres porcelain service, we often sit on the table.

While the waitress caressed Bill's exposed neck, just at that exact nano second, as I turned around to make myself comfortable on the table top, taking a moment to look over the room, just then, out of the corner of my eye, I saw a huge hairy hand sweep by my eyes, grab me by the scruff of my neck, and throw me like a bag of rubbish onto the sawdust covered floor. I rolled over in the cigarettes, cigar butts, blood, spit, and dirty, beer damp sawdust, and came up with the man's ankle in my teeth.

Bill looked over in shock, jumped up, and at the same moment, in a huge arcing uppercut, hit the man in his ugly face with the back of his hand. He shook his hand, pretending like it hurt when he hit the man hard on his nose.

Bill looked at the man who was now streaming blood from his perhaps broken nose, and said in a whiny voice I recognized from Bill's childhood and his brutal mother's mocking, "Iz ow widdle nosey unhappy?"

Then Bill pulled the bleeding man close to him, and kneed him in the balls. The guy dropped like a stone to the floor, writhing in pain. Bill stood over him like Muhammad Ali stood over George Foreman in their famous "Rumble in the Jungle."

Remember here, Bill was a sizable man raised his whole life in logging camps. Bill knew how to fight dirty or clean. He told the guy writhing on the floor if he ever touched his dog again, he would kick his ass so far up around his shoulders he would have to part his hair to take a shit.

Bill never did, nor would he ever, hit his parents, no matter how much they abused him. So tough, so strong, he had been in many fights, yet so meek. Make no mistake, he could hold his own in a fight, fair or dirty, but that wasn't the case in this place. It was him against the whole crowd. He was an outsider with a dog that sat on the table.

At the same moment the man hit the floor one of the guy's friends hit Bill on his temple with a clear plastic ice crusher, the ones on bar tops with steel gears imbedded in their bottoms.

As Bill fell, groaning, I sunk my teeth into the guy's ankle harder until I hit his bone with my long incisors. I could taste his metallic, unhappy blood.

I growled and thought, "Iz r widdle ankle unhappy?"

Three of their other friends came and picked us up, and with lots of shouts and curses and threats, threw us out into the gravel parking lot. I didn't mention this before but I believe I may have broken one of the creep's little fingers when he picked me up to throw me out the door.

Well that was quite an exit.

Bill lay in the parking lot face down

where they had thrown him groaning and bleeding long after they slammed the door and went back into the bar. Bill finally came around, woke up, pushed himself up on his hands and knees, and stood unsteadily to his feet. We climbed in the Cuda and sat for sometime. After Bill got his bearings as we sat there it started to lightly snow.

Sitting in Bill's lap we quietly sat there a while, then Bill, finally coming around some, said, "What the hell just happened?"

We sat there until the same group, drunker now, came out and told us to get the hell out of there or they would call the Sheriff.

The guy that I had bitten was bleeding through his pants on his ankle, the other guy I had bit on the hand had it wrapped in a bloody handkerchief. One of the other guys had a large, blood soaked gauze bandage on his nose.

He pounded on the window, leaving

a bloody mark, and yelled, "That son of a bitch of a dog of yours should have a muzzle, and a team of lawyers, and you should be in jail! Get the hell out of here now, you hear me? And I mean NOW."

We found a wide grassy snowy place out by a dark river with large stones in the center capped with rich green moss. As it lightly snowed, each mossy rock was gradually forming a chapeau of the brightest white of neige, or snow for those of you who speak no French.

We sat out there in the dark, the head lights shinning out over the river, the deep mountains and forest dimly visible on the other side.

It was one of those snow falls that falls straight down. It fell into the strong smooth flowing river where it instantly dissolved. Soon as the snow hit the river it was gone and became part of the river. Whats the French saying, "you never step into the same river twice."

We sat a while, the blood clotted on Bill's face, and between you and me, Bill looked like hell. The whole side of his face was black and blue. We watched the snow falling hypnotically into the void.

The car was warm. It was cold outside. I know it was cold since it was snowing when we both got out to pee. Cold!

The Cuda's heater was humming, the radio playing "Take Five," Dave Brubeck's classic. Bill got out the bottle of Jack Daniel's he had bought at a convenience store and took three long swallows. All I could do was shudder and think of his alcoholic parents, but then I hadn't been smashed on the side of my head by an ice crusher. Whiskey had its place from time to time.

We had some white bread that had molded itself into a distorted mass, but still edible, smeared with yellow mustard in a little squat jar. There was a chunk of hard sausage and slightly moldy yellow cheese, a beef bone and some canned dog food. I had water in a little plastic plate. Bill steadily drank Jack to dull his temple pain. We slept in the car, Bill moaning all night from the beating.

Sleeping in the car was cold. We slept in the back seat, me wrapped in Bill's black and green checked loggers jacket. It smelled rich, sweaty, and earthy inside the jacket dark like a burrow. I love this man.

At some point in the early night a car pulled up beside us and stopped. A guy rolled down his window and held out a pistol pointing toward the sky and cocked it.

Bill rolled down the Cuda window, held up his chrome Smith and Wesson 38, and yelled at the guy, "I've got one too, with hollow points." The guy drove away.

The wind came up in the early morning while it was still nearly dark. Then I heard rain falling on the leaves in the nearby forest, and sank back into deep sleep from my bed under the back window. When I awoke again, the rain had stopped and it was quiet, very still, silent.

I noticed the windows were covered again with snow. When Bill opened the door, some snow fell inside the Cuda, we found we were in a white wonder world with large snow flakes majestically floating like white silver dollars out of grey pewter skies.

Bill scooped some snow from the hood of the Cuda and held it to his black and blue temple.

We drove all that day and the next evening we arrived some place in the middle of a large port city. The snow had turned to slush. There were fog horns from ships out in the great grey galvanized harbor. Distant headlands were equally indistinct.

Bill shouted to me in the back seat where I was sleeping, "Seattle, Frankie. This is Seattle, Washington, United States of America." Then he laughed.

Have you ever been to Seattle? Every street ends at some dead end waterway. The whole town is hills, valleys, bays, lakes, rivers, locks, and steamer docks.

There is a seam of homeless blue tented encampments running through the city like blue mold in a loaf of gorgonzola. A seam of these blue tents connected Alaska Way, running along the water front. We found ourselves in this blur of blue and dogs and grocery carts filled with trash. There were garbage cans and overflowing cardboard boxes of junk, wheel chairs on their sides, pallets and propane tanks, all in some major state of disarray. Through this unhealthy confusion, people in various states of dress and undress smoked, vaped, and sat in dejected lumps. The whole of it was filled with a greenish miasma. One or two places stood out, the Edgewater Inn for one, while h covering over the whole wet homeless mess was the inspiring space needle. Seattle's last great moment was its world's fair.

We didn't know up from down, one street was as good as another since we really had no final destination except Seattle, which was pretty big we soon found out.

We drove on by and around water ways and lakes, hills and tunnels, and got completely confused. Dead ends, private gated neighborhoods, government property, it started to look all the same.

It was maybe eleven at night and incessantly raining. Bill's black and blue temple was throbbing.

Driving out toward a place Bill pointed out was named Ballard, I looked out the wind and rain runneled windows, and everywhere I looked there were crates, crab traps, forklifts, stacks of nets, and stacks of lumber and engine parts. It is beyond me, this desert rat, how anyone could live in a place this cold and washed out. It all looked so bleak.

Seattle is an old black and white photograph.

After driving up this street and down another street we arrived, unknown to us, at a place called Fisherman's Terminal, a place that would change our lives forever.

What Bill and I thought was a road turned out to be a dock that, when we drove over it, made a blunk blunk noise. A sign said dead end, keep out. Behind an open gate on the wooden dock, Bill spied a place by some stacked equipment where we could park for the night in a shadow, more or less private and out of sight, or so we thought. There were feeble yellow single lights here and there, swinging in the driving rain.

I watched a sopping wet black cat running in the dark with a kitten in her mouth.

Parking in the lee of a tall stack of empty pallets, Bill shut down the popping hot

426, and said, "We are as far north in the lower forty-eight as we can go, ole pal, unless we take a boat to Alaska."

He laughed and said, "Unlikely that's happening. We had a piece of beef jerky, and sat chewing, listening to the rain pounding on the roof. "God what a place", Bill muttered. Well good night, Frankie, sleep tight we will see what tomorrow brings ." His temple and face were still black and blue.

With that we both crawled into the spacious back seat. I jumped up on my velvet ledge beneath the rear window while Bill curled up under a blanket after first tucking me in under his wool knit sweater. I lay there awhile, a sad orange beam of light sliced through the car into my eyes until I turned over. I lay there a while thinking about the day Bill killed the wolf. Someone said cats have nine lives, dogs twelve. That wolf had only one. Today he was feeding the fishes. I went into a peaceful sleep as rain pelted the canvas top of the Cuda. Sometime in the night the rain stopped.

I was dreaming of a beautiful boat in a violent storm, then six or eight small grey-brown marbled owls, the kind that roosted in the trees in the high Sierras, flooded into my stormy dream. The owls kept coming and landing in front of me, then when I got close they flew, only to come back again and again. Sort of like falling in a dream and never hitting the bottom of anything, only endless falling.

Suddenly, a cold windy shadow passed over my dream, like a dream super imposed over another dream, like a fog with many misplaced objects super imposed on each other, distant and near. When I am frightened in a dream I can wake myself up. This I did.

I opened my eyes in the early morning grey looking out and stared right into the eyes of an old man in a slouchy hat and coat, the stub of a glowing cigarette in his slack mouth. I rushed at the window and in the process I awakened Bill with my full throated vicious snarling. Bill looked and saw me looking at a dark old man standing in the leaden rain with his face close to the wet, cold, fog-smeared window looking into the Cuda.

I barked my loudest, and at the same moment, the old man pounded on the window and yelled, "This is private property, or didn't you see the god damned sign, now get your asses the hell out of here. Jesus, everywhere I look I see you homeless friggin' bums."

Bill groggily opened the car door. As he stepped out into the rain which had started to fall again, I also jumped out, but remember, I am trained. I didn't bark or bite. I did softly growl though. I am a dog after all.

"What the hell are you parking here for? This city is plugged with people like you.

Blue tents everywhere, wasting my time and my money. What I am doing is called work, though you probably wouldn't know what that is. Nobody seems to work anymore, shit. Last week I threw to bastards like you out through that gate, what are you waiting for, get back in that purple wreck of yours and leave, now!

"What the hell is wrong with your face? Black and blue, is that all you bums do is beat up on each other? The bums I threw out last week had needle marks, their arms were black and blue, what the hell is humanity coming to?"

"Are you hard of hearing? See that boat over the other side of the dock? Well I've got to get that loaded and ready for Cordova, Alaska. Though if I had to make a guess I wouldn't know Cordova Alaska from your right bun. I don't even know why I am talking to you. I've got a time limit, it's called the tide. To quote an old saw, 'The tide waits for no man, however many a man has waited for the tide.' Now get the hell out of here. Go find people like yourselves in some tent city, you will find them and a hopeless hovel near anywhere in this god forsaken city.

God damn it, Son, you look like a decent enough kid, I've boys myself.

One last thing I'll say to you, my wife says all of you bums have names and mothers. What's your name and where is your mother? And by the way, is that your mutt?"

"Ya," Bill said like he was ashamed of me.

"So for the last time, move your God damn car. Why am I wasting my time? You are blocking that load of engine parts. "Hey Trigve" he yelled at a guy driving by, "get that damn fork lift over here, soon as this guy moves his car and get these pallets over to the Lynch, pronto. The big crated cats first, then the rest. Next he turned to Bill and said,

"you know anything at all, Son?"

"No," Bill mumbled, hanging his head down while looking away.

"That's what I thought. Get your God damn dog back in the car and clear out. What the hell, everywhere you look you see bums in rags and blue tents. You probably have a blue tent yourself. Why don't you people ever work, get a job, support yourselves, instead sucking at the government tit? Hard working people like me have to support people like you."

"I pay my way," said Bill. "I never took a government dime in my life, God damn it."

"Tell me this," the old guy said. "How does someone living in their god damned car pay their way, hum? Answer me that." Obviously you got no home!

"Well, sleeping in my car don't mean I don't work, nor does it mean I can't work.

I work, same as you." Then Bill said, "I'm a top man, a high forest logging rigger, I spend my days on nylon threads like a spider 100 feet off of the forest floor. That is work and son of a bitch if I ain't good at it.

"So, while I am on my rant and at it with some heat at your insults, let me tell you this since you are kicking us out of here anyway, and I've had time to look things over, I should tell you this out of the kindness of my bleeding heart. I've met plenty just like you, you old codger. I don't pretend to know shit about fishing or navigating a tub like your barge there, but I know a hell of a lot more about rigging than the sorry son of a bitch who ever created that rat's nest sort of, ya that right sort of, lashed down to your deck. Whoever rigged those pallets knows nothing about tie downs and rigging. First puff, that load is going to be all over the deck, if not floating all over the damn North Pacific. You can't release those granny knots in an emergency. But then I'm guessing you don't know shit from shineola about knots, my guess you couldn't tell a bowline knot from a rolling hitch from a square knot. That deck load is dangerous. So don't say I never did anything for you," said Bill. "That deck load needs to be redone, plain and simple as the nose on your face. There, you can have that advice for the rent of your crappy dock last night, and it wasn't even all night, ol' timer. By the way, continue the way you are loading and when you slack the lines, you are going to be listing to the right, or as you say on the water, the starboard, about 10-12 degrees." But then what ever lout loaded it didn't, obviously take that into account, weight matters, and where and how it is loaded as important on a log truck or a tub like yours there.

Bill turned to the old guy and said, "Get that damn forklift out of my way so I can get hell out of here."

I looked up at Bill and thought to myself, "My God, this is a new Bill. What has just happened to make this change?" Where has he been hiding or did he just get to the place in life where it was stand up or lie down? He was standing tall. In life there are lots of choices. Every cause produces more than one effects, and I know this as well, you belong to the power you choose to obey. It's a choice, some dogs are weak, whine and whimper while others are strong great intelligent companions that take no bull shit or any kind of shit for that matter. Your home is the place you live your life, make it count. Humans are no different, and Bill?

well here is a thought, maybe it started when he finally summoned up the courage to walk out on his mother. He decided he wasn't going to belong to her twisted power any more. Make a choice.

"Ok, ok, wait a minute, the old guy back off. Maybe I was a bit hasty, maybe even nasty. What say we shake and start all over? I have a lot of pressure on me right now to set sail, sometimes it brings out the worst in me, so my wife tells me," and he kind of laughed then coughed, the spit. "They call me Smitty, what's your handle, and who's your side kick?"

At that Bill picked me up and while holding me he shook Smitty's hand, then took my paw and I shook Smitty's hand as well. Smitty laughed and scratched me under my chin on my breast bone, which if you know anything about dogs you must know we all love that. Still for me, there was something about this guy that was just a click off.

"I need a first mate. My old first mate is up town on a bender and I fired him last night. He was no good anyway. You know by now I am the skipper of this tub, as you call her, though we call her the Cape Lynch. I need a first mate," started Smitty. "Someone who can do lots of different jobs, and it seems like you might fill that bill. I can teach you to navigate. We are supposed to be shoving off for Alaska to Prince William Sound tomorrow. Cash money at the end of the season when we arrive back here in Seattle after the summer season." During the season you have free chow and a place to sleep of your own.

"I've got my dog, Frankie," said Bill.

"Take him to the pound. They will find a place for him right away. He's pretty damn cute."

"You know Captain Smitty, you can shit and fall back in it. That there dog and I have been through hell, though I am guessing you wouldn't know what kind of hell I'm talking about. Here is how it lines out: he goes or I stay."

Smitty looked Bill over with a little more respect and said, "Jesus, a little tightly wound, aren't you? Ok, you can bring him.

By the way, we have got a large Ragdoll calico cat on board, too."

"I've got a car, a damn good one too," Bill said.

"Empty it out and we will put it in the warehouse, you can pick it up when we return. The warehouse is secure." When Trygve moves the pallets you can park there where you are and we can talk. After we talk and I think you can do the job, you can start today. We slept there that night.

The next morning standing in the wheelhouse of the Cape Lynch, Smitty stood with his scrawny arm hooked around a spoke on the large wooden ship's wheel.

"Ok, let's start again with what you can do. Has anyone taught you how to do anything? Did you graduate from high school? Can you write? What I want to know is what do you know, what are your skills?"

Bill said, "I can drop a two hundred foot tall redwood on a rocky hillside on a toothpick, though," Bill chuckled here, "I don't think you will be wanting me to do that.

"Beside that I took night classes and have a college degree in writing. I'm a certified heavy machinery diesel, as well as gas, mechanic. I cut my teeth working on large diesel engines since I was strong enough to hold a socket wrench. I had my own dragster, it was very quick, it had a Chevy 7.0 liter V-8 small block LS7 engine. I nearly died in it. My purple Cuda out there has a 426 in it, which I do all the mechanical on it. I can weld, tig, mig, wire feed, aluminum, steel stainless steel, plasma cutters, oxyacetylene cutters, pretty much anything to do with heavy or light metal. I can rivet as well.

"My grandfather had me pumping a blacksmith forge for him when I was so small I had to stand on a cut stump to reach the blower handle. I can weld in a forge, which pretty much nobody can do that anymore. I have a CDL license, I can run and repair any kind of hydraulics, I have endless hours on any kind of crane, including the ones here on the Lynch.

I can rig anything on the deck, as well as work off the deck. I can work a spread sheet for keeping records, which neither of my parents could do.

"I'm a pretty decent logger style cook. I like sharpened saws, I like clean bunks. If a guy can't even keep his own bed, how can he organize the rest of his life?

I demand a clean kitchen with sharp knives. I like clean toilets and sinks."

Bill chuckled a moment and said, "What is it about people? They want to change the world, but won't change the toilet paper roll.

"I worked in logging camps my whole life. I'm use to loggers personal habits, and I don't suppose fishermen are much different. Don't ask me to paint! By the way, Smitty, I see your dock men are still loading this barge the same way. Mark my words, she will be listing."

Bill emptied out the Cuda and we found our stateroom right behind the door up a short set of steps to the wheelhouse. My favorite spot in the wheelhouse was by the binnacle. It was warm. The binnacle gently rolled this way and that, its brass and archaic golden writing, with its dim penumbraed signs and icons, somehow were reassuring. In the sunlight its warm brass surface was warm on my hair. This little whirling bit of liquid and gimbals could and did lead us through the darkest nights.

However those days of loss and darkness were in the future. This was the day we had, and it was mostly drudgery for everyone on board.

As we neared the end of the last departure day, everyone worked a little harder, a little faster, to batten down the hatches, making ready to depart at 1700 hours. We also had the final opening of the Ballard Bridge for the night. We needed to make it at 1730 hours or spend another night in Ballard. This meant that our parent company would be changed an extra night by all of the crew, a major no no. We had the compass spun, the booms lowered and secured, by Bill, we had the decks washed down, the windows washed, fuel tanks topped off, water tanks filled, and finally groceries, frozen meats and fresh produce were delivered on board.

As we were finally slamming the wedges home over the canvas cover fore deck, a circus like band of jovial, as in drunk, people, in number 10 or 12, all of Smitty's family from the country, cascaded on board with baskets of food, kids, a large old lethargic dog, and booze, lots of booze. They all smoked, some rolled their own. One older man, helped on board, crippled, sat on the hatch top and smoked an old fashioned pipe that curved down over his chin. He had the stem wrapped with white halibut twine so as to better hold it in his mouth where he had few teeth. His little nephew continuously set little glasses beside him filled with amber liquid.

Smitty stepped up on the guard rail and rolled himself a cigarette while his happy chubby wife placed a large iced Jack and Coke in his waiting hand. He danced a little reel. I couldn't imagine how he could do it, but he did. Then after finishing several more glasses of Jack, polishing off chicken wings, parts of steaks, torn chunks of bread, he toasted everyone, even me, and the dreaming somnambulant dog who gave an old wet righteous cough.

For the next hour everyone was shouting, "Alaska or bust!" while swilling down copious amounts of whisky and vodkas and Coke.

One of the kids had made a flag with a skull and cross bones to fly from our mast head, he then climbed on top of the wheel-house and hoisted his skull and cross bones up our mast over the American flag.

They were all, every last one of them, our whole crew, completely drunk. Smitty's fat wife was passed out in the galley where she had thrown up on the galley seating benches. Drinks were poured and forgotten, half consumed glasses of various liquors lined the rails on the afterdeck. Also here and there were partially eaten foods, rolls of sausage, yellow cheese, loaves of bread, cracked crab, smoked salmon. One of Smitty's aunts rolled him a joint. She was expert at rolling finely made joints. She slowly, while winking at Smitty, rolled a perfect torpedo and slipped it into his shirt pocket. Everyone was drunk and stoned and very happy.

I was fed copious amounts of cold T-bone steak, bones and all, and smoked fish, which I love by the way, sort of reminds me of the French Concale oysters. Smitty fired up the afterdeck speakers and everyone started to dance. A very colorful assortment of drunks, each of them right out of Hogarth, nearly everyone was a red head. Some had clog shoes. They slapped their thighs. This group liked to drink. This group liked to squaller. This group like to drink off of the government tit. The eagle flies on Friday. Oh, they had been to the Puyallup fair and left their dignity God knows where.

Drunkenness, like infinity, is a fenceless boundary.

Just when everyone was at their most joyous drunkenness, when the old dog finally was on his splayed feet licking the oyster shells on the deck, when the little six year old was licking the brass rail on the way up to the wheelhouse stair way, just when young Angus pulled out his fiddle and everyone began to dance, when they were drunk, sick, happy beyond compare, just then, that moment, an ogre, tall, forbidding, with a tattered long dark seaman's coat, a high collar hiding his long extenuated neck, his face sallow, dark, appeared at the foot of the gang plank looking at the riotous assemblage with monstrous hideous distain. He turned and spit into the quiet oily grey water, the reflective water at the side of the Cape Lynch. His spit was yellow-green.

He was a tall, erect old man, darkly dressed, his hat a slouchy deep brown bowler. It was pulled low against the weather and all of humanity. As he pulled one boney pale hand against the railing he slowly pulled his way up the gang plank. It was easy to see he was painfully dragging his right foot. Did you ever see a dog hit by a car? He looked like he had been hit by life, and was deeply wounded. Maybe he would survive, and maybe he wouldn't.

Half way up the gang plank he stopped and looked at all of the drunken merriment, turned, and spit into the lake canal again.

He happened to look over and see me sitting on the rail and sort of awkwardly smiled at me, and tried to pat me on the head. He missed. Muttering to himself, he asked one of the kids for Smitty, then asked Smitty for the number of his stateroom.

Smitty jocularly said to him, "Friend, it is number two in the passage on the port side."

The old cook, for indeed this was the cook, looked Smitty in the eye and I said, "I ain't your yer friend. Is something funny?"

Then the old sour man, painfully, coughing, scowling, darkly, slowly, so slowly, purposefully disappeared like an old grizzly with bad teeth, slamming the door hand behind him.

Just before disappearing into his cabin, he shouted gruffly, loudly, hoarsely, at everyone on the deck, "Shut up, you bastards," as if sometime in his lonely life he was used to being obeyed.

This time though, everyone was drunk and loud and paid him no attention. Little did we know that was the last of him we would see until Ketchikan.

This event woke Smitty up, who looked at his pocket watch, "Oh shit," and yelled to anyone who would listen, "Everybody off, we are leaving NOW!"

No one got off. His family was everywhere on the Cape Lynch like maggots in a piece of rotten beef. Some in the forward bunks passed out, his wife still sick in the galley. His little thirteen year old nephew was on top of the wheelhouse, smoking a joint, his old relative with the pipe was passed out cold on the fore hatch. His aunt was chain smoking joints on the afterdeck.

Spotting Trigve our engineer, he yelled down from the wheelhouse, "Fire the cats, we are leaving now."

When Trig didn't move, Smitty threw a

hamburger bun at him, yelling, "Now, God damn it! the Ballard Bridge closes in moments! Now, now!"

Trigve jumped, shouting, "Ya dooo," and raced below to the engine room.

On the way past the afterdeck he stopped at Smitty's aunt sitting on the after rail, had two quick puffs of her joint, and raced below to the engine room.

He ignited the twin D17000 Caterpillar engines. As he did so black diesel smoke poured into the misty, foggy, early evening sky.

Smitty yelled, "Let go aft."

One of Smitty's nephews pulled the stern line while Bill waited for Smitty's command, then pulled the bow line. He looked at the dark dirty diesel emitting from the stacks and shook his head. He knew the engines were not tuned right, and neither of them was collimated with the other. Remember, his whole life was large diesel engines.

Sure as hell as soon as the lines were released the old Lynch listed about ten degrees to the starboard, Bill looked up at Smitty standing in the open window of the wheel house.

Smitty slowly eased the port control forward while he pulled the starboard control back.

The old Cape Lynch slowly, ponderously turned herself in her length and pulled her bulk sideways out into the waterway. A trail of rainbow colored oil drifted off of the hull as she edged out, leaving the grey tattered dock. Smitty slowly eased, pushed both controls into forward while the Cape Lynch evened out, ponderously heading down the crowded waterway-canal toward the Ballard Bridge, the Government Locks, Puget Sound, where the wide North Pacific lay broadly and distantly ahead, and finally Alaska.

We were late for the bridge, Smitty knew it. He goosed the Lynch to eight knots in a waterway that was state and federally strictly restricted to five knots to keep from swamping moored boats along the way as well as damaging docks and other floating and non floating objects. The Lynch, with her ponderous bulk, blunt bow in the small confines of the canal, started to throw a steep wake which bounced and rolled from one side of the narrow concrete canal to the other behind us.

It took a long distance to stop the Lynch. We were in a narrow, concrete lined canal with boats and house boats large and small lining the concrete margins.

Owners of these boats and house boats were shouting and cursing, shaking their fists, giving us the finger, as we powered past this chorus of angry people, yelling, "Slow down, you bastards!"

The Lynches' blunt barge-like bow in

this small confined waterway threw a herculean wake, a not-so-mini tsunami. As we approached the Ballard Bridge at eight knots we could all see that the bridge was starting to close for the night. Its last opening by the government clock now past. Smitty, drunk and stoned, his nephews crowding the wheelhouse, his wife vomiting off the rail, pushed the controls further, goosing the Lynch to nine knots, top speed for the old scow.

The bridge tender was blowing five shorts on his whistle, which meant to immediately reverse engines. We were listing at 12 degrees to the starboard, and just as the bridge was closing we were at the perfect angle to slide between the two closing jaws of the bear trap steel girded bridge.

The bridge tender came out of his control booth and yelled at Smitty and gave him the finger, with both hands.

Smitty, still at nine knots, being drunk

and stoned, approached the tie up bollards for the Government Locks, swamping and leaving small boats behind us roiling and rocking.

We approached the bollards lining the locks so fast we ground our truck tire fenders into the concrete walls until they smoked black acrid smoke which enveloped the lock in a midnight petrol cloud. One of the tires caught fire by friction for a moment, then went out by itself.

Smitty, completely inebriated, got confused and hit reverse on the starboard engine instead of the port engine and swung us almost sideways in the lock.

The lock attendant was beside himself as we drifted into a gravel barge. The skipper of the gravel barge gave Smitty the finger with both hands.

Smitty, with the help of his two 12 year old twin nephews, finally managed to get straight in the lock, tied and secure. Smitty's whole drunken family jumped, stumbled, and fell from the boat onto the concrete lock deck. This is completely and federally forbidden. You go to prison for this. Absolutely no boarding or departing a vessel while in the locks. The lock captain was livid, cursing Smitty and his family while they all scurried and stumbled away into the drunken dark rain for all the world looking like a pack of oily compromised rats.

The Lynch slowly settled from the upper water level of Lake Washington down 20 feet to the level of Puget Sound, and as such to the level of the surface of the entire earth's oceans.

The large dripping lock doors, covered in green algae, in slow-motion swung open while the briny saline waters from the Salish sea swirled in and around the Lynch. She jerked and pulled gently at her lines as the salt water flowed in, displacing the lake water.

From high above our deck up on top by the bollard a voice shouted down to us, "Look alive down there," and expertly dropped our lines onto our decks, bow and stern.

"By the way," he shouted down to us, "I'm not putting in a complaint. I also heard from the bridge tender, you sure as hell need one. Get your act together. The ocean's not kind to stupidity."

Then he turned to his left and spit into the empty lock.

Smitty pushed both controls forward and the D17000s rumbled, echoing deeply in the cavernous lock as we slowly picked up speed, entering Puget Sound heading north.

The sense that we were out of a fresh-water lake and onto the briny ocean was immediately apparent: seagulls, seals, diving sea ducks, tugs lined up to load the lock going up into the lake. Looking out across our bow we could see Bainbridge Island and Puget Sound extending far into the rainy evening in the rain soaked misted distance.

Bill coiled the lines and made the decks shipshape, and then climbed the rain wet ladder with me under his strong arm to the wheelhouse. The cook's door was closed, the engineer's door was also closed. Smitty, severely hung over from his debauch all day, slouched at the large wooden ships wheel. The D17000 cats murmured away, rain pelted the windows which were just cracked open at their tops to let in fresh air. Smitty's vacuous stoned eyes were half closed. The iron mike, our auto pilot, whined away with each change in direction as we began our long journey north.

As Bill and I came up into the wheelhouse, Bill took a seat up by the chart table, I jumped up into his lap. After an hour or so in the silent quiet warm wheelhouse, with only the whine of the iron mike to break the thick alcoholic silence, Smitty stumbled over to Bill and started to teach him a bit about navigation, at least the navigating this our beginning day would require, if not demand, since the crew was not available. They were passed out.

Turning to the chart table, Smitty pointed back to the entrance to the Ballard Locks where we had entered into Puget Sound on the marine chart. "Thats our departure point, then turning he pointed up sound and that's where we are heading."

Heading north up Admiralty Inlet, Smitty said, "See the light off the port side, way up in the distance past that blue freighter heading south? That's Apple Tree Point.

"By the way Smitty slurred, most water ways in the civilized world have buoys indicating when ships and marine traffic are entering port and leaving port, all these buoys defining very important waterways. Here on Puget Sound, and most places in the world, at their very must basic, the maritime rules of the road are 'Red Right Returning'. That means at the entrance to each harbor there will be a red can buoy, often with a red light. You always keep the 'Red Can' to your right when entering Port. When leaving the port outward-bound, obviously the red can will be on your port side.

"When we reach the entrance to Friday Harbor, keep a sharp look out starboard for the red can with its steadily flashing red light." Dully looking around the wheelhouse, Smitty said to Bill, "We have gone over this, so you ok with it?"

"Ya" said Bill. "By the way, 'Point No Point' flashes three whites every ten seconds, that's it out there to the port, correct?"

"That's right, you got her, Skipper. Goodnight.

"By the way, one last important thing. Here today we are northbound, port light to port light, starboard is green, port is red.

If the port light, red, of another boat or ship is passing you it means the other ship is trending out of your path. If the red light is visible at the same time as the starboard light, coming right at you, listen carefully now, this is very important, and you can see both red and green starboard light, the other boat is on a collision coarse with you coming directly at you. Sound your horn, five short blasts, blat, blat, blat, blat, blat, and turn starboard rapidly away from the projected path of the other boat.

"Trust your navigational equipment, but verify with your own eyes. The normal procedure is turn hard to starboard on a collision course, unless, important here, unless that turns you into the path of the on coming vessel. Be alert."

Smitty slurred his words, sat down on the wheelhouse stool, stood up, went out on the bridge wing, and peed over the side. Then, coming back in, stumbled on the threshold and fell into Bill's strong young arms.

Pulling Smitty upright, Bill said, "I can do this. Hit the hay, Skipper, you have had a long day."

Smitty lowered one of the side windows a few inches, reached into his pocket for the joint his aunt had given him at the dock, torched it, took a few puffs, snuffed it out, and put the butt back into his pocket.

Smitty said to Bill, "Take the wheel, call me when you get to Cattle Point on San Juan Island. That will be about six hours at seven knots." Smitty stoped with one foot over the threshold and chuckled, "God damn, we pissed 'em all off today."

Walking out, he quietly closed the mahogany wheelhouse door.

Bill picked me up sat me up by the compass in front of the great wooden steering wheel. Up there I looked out over the fore hold and bow.

Small windshield wipers vainly tried to keep the windows clear of misty rain, but then there wasn't much to run into. Waves were nudging the Lynch to the northeast as we were picked up by waves from our port quarter slightly skewed. It was warm and comfortable in the wheelhouse. My cushion was down filled. We had red lights on in the wheelhouse at night, as well as the instrument panels. This way your eyes were always acclimated to the dark. White light in the wheelhouse destroys your night vision.

As Bill began to learn to steer he zigged and zagged his way up Puget Sound. When he zigged, the golden compass tipped one way, and when he zagged, it tilted the other way. Its dim soft little light lit the antique golden compass title written in its old fashion scroll. Like me with my nose, I am locked when on scent and direction. So also is the Lynch's compass, with the Cape Lynch at its center. We spin and we whirl, but somehow the compass always points us north on course, point no point five miles up sound.

Heavy obscuring rain-dark at twilight, dull dreary grey sea sky, light airs, as we passed Point Partridge to our immediate starboard, at 2000 hours." I watched as Bill turned from the wheel, facing the chart table and write and entry in the log book

Slowly, while rain slashed our windows, from quick little intense showers of rain, day turned to night with a broad array of distant flashing and steady glowing lights beginning to show themselves around us. Looking out our port wheelhouse door I could see the red glow of the port light reflected on the white of the exterior wheelhouse. Looking out the starboard wheelhouse door I could see the reflective glow of the green starboard light.

As twilight deepened, reality changed to fantasy, to castles and drifting islands of fog. Lights and horns spun in a kaleido-scope around our moving boat.

There were flashing lights of distant low stars and criss crossing patterns of red and green air craft. The night time maritime world changed to light pulses that must be heeded. This was where faith and experience take hold. It was here that your instruments must be accurate. Think of sea lights at night in a boat as a school of neon tetra, they never run into each other, we humans do. The lights were glowing in round lighted holes in the dense dark, tall slow paced sailboat's mast lights show up shadowy and airy and moving very slowly in the dark, we see especially sailboats and log booms on the radar way before we sight them by eye.

Everyone is going a different speed and a different direction. Passing cruise ships, great glutted blobs of humanity that they are, a slice of Manhattan in day and night, a Mississippi riverboat alive as a cake with a thousand candles. Freighters and ferry boats all lit in different ways. What makes visual sighting so difficult at night is the ability to see if an object is distant or right up close. Is it moving or still?

That medicine thing called luck. Lucks a chance, however you have to have prepared your Ju Ju so that out there you can discern that there is no floating log, or ship, or large object dark, and without power, this is where the compass and radar are your indispensable guides. They were checked, calibrated before you threw off the lines in Seattle, this was mandatory. It takes great attention to believe you see something that is not on the radar. Water does strange things, when you swear you see a foaming rock filled surf ahead of you, checking your radar and charts, you hold your breath, sweat blood, go gasping out onto the bridge with glasses to see if you are about to run into a ragged coast of foaming surf. Experience tells you stay the course.

The edges of the sea are hard, unyielding, a constant dangerous source of surprise. The whole Pacific Coast up the inside, in fact the entire maritime world, is littered with ship wrecks by men and women who made the wrong choices. Luck such a bug-a-boo, such a trickster, it does sadistic things, It does humorous things, it ambushes you, it seduces you, luck is such a bug-a-boo.

Tides play serious tricks, with your eyes, your perceptions, your motions, tides give you vertigo as they slip sideways by and around you. They rise and fall over 18 feet in some places.

Rocks nicely covered at one tidal stage of 15 feet of water are at another stage same rocks only covered by six inches of hard, deathly, unyielding basalt, the knife edge of the inner earth. You often don't see this in calm weather.

You can read the surface of the sea like a book, in fact it is a book, it's open pages filled with words of a different language. The surface of the book called the ocean, is constantly moving, from flat calm to gale force winds and everything in between, it is constantly changing colors, the ocean is the earths largest mirror. What happens in the sky is reflected in the sea. Run head on into swells, your boat jumps and slams, use a different approach and quarter the waves and you will have a smooth ride. Perhaps the word of the day in your ocean book, is cloud. The clouds to the weather are like adjectives, they are indicators, modifiers, they tell the beginning of a story, or perhaps the end of a story, such as distant large swells from a now long gone storm in the deep Pacific. Clouds scud along the surface as fog, maybe the current is going one direction and the wind another, the mariner must be able to read any and all of this, this is called experience. If a mariner cannot read the winds, the tides, the clouds, the surface of the sea, they are the most likely to drown at the upper limit or get the hell beaten out of them and the lower extreme.

Maybe you are in the midst of a chaotic bucket of oceanic waves going every which way, called a confused sea. No matter what course you choose, the ride is rough. As my old grandfather Christophe use to say, " Prepare for trouble, for lucks a chance but trouble's sure."

Some time you might see a very subtle rolling v-shaped wave on calm water holding steady softly splitting the water causing a soft subtle wake while a light current flows around it. If you see this avoid it for beneath that soft fold lies an unyielding kelp covered stone, it is a noun, a basaltic hard noun, in the ocean's book. The water may look twelve feet deep out over your bow, but if you look at your chart or your

Fathometer, you discover it is 4 feet deep, low water.

Danger lurks everywhere, gouging, splitting, splintering wrenching danger feasts on the innocent and the careless. The bottom of the inside passage is not a flat ball room floor or a blank page. It is mountainous, some of the mountain's peaks rise to and through the surface, while some at the lowest tide hoover inches down. These may give an indication on the calm surface, but then you must know how to read that adjective. There are great canyons, hot springs, and tunnels. To navigate this oceanic book, you need a speed reading course. Quick response to what you are "reading" is essential, to miss the critical lesson, that moment, can be dire.

Sailors must not hit the shore, do not cut points, do not get into broaching seas, go slowly in fog, do not ever go to sleep on wheel watch, stay in assigned channels.

Read the book the sea presents to you, study hard, understand it, your life depends on it.

The sea is not a place to go wandering without knowing what lies beneath those oh so innocent looking calm waters. Look you may comment , at the reflective clouds and blue skies, an innocent blanketed reflection covering a desperate world of various desperate primacies. Terror reigns among the fishes, while the inky dark shore at night is forbidding from the wheel house..

Sailing at night assumes, demands alertness on the part of the mariner.

Bill was very, in fact, highly alert, however this world of the sea was a foreign world from toping trees in the high Sierras. However, there were many similarities. The men for one were very similar, the danger was similar, the food was similar, the sleeping conditions were similar.

One simple small point that isn't similar is this: logging is not done at night. Life on the sea goes on day and night, in all kinds of weather and light, as well as at extreme tides at all stages over rocks covered by a foot of water or 14 feet.

Sometimes mother nature and Neptune are beneficent, even looking kindly, even fatherly on fools at sea. However, Neptune is a serious taskmaster. Remember the sequence of lights, don't ever get off a light. If you get lost, shut down and drift until you find out where the hell you are. Don't temp fate, this is a fools game over and over and over as old as man's first voyage on the sea. Neptune may shake his Trident at the sky, look, read the clouds where he is pointing. Mother Nature may send little innocent soft cat's paws before a hurricane, a warning, be alert.

Sailing the dark inside passage, if one is off by one, only one, winkling, twinkling innocent flashing white light, two shorts every 15 seconds, if you get off that single light, only providence can save you from sailing into oblivion. If you zig instead of zag you are most surly lost. Death comes fast, suffocating wetness unending, senescence quickly, not a life time of slow memory loss, near instantaneously. As the sea, the oh so beautiful rolling sea, folds over you, all memory is erased. Finis.

Bill was overjoyed standing tall at the wheel. How, he wondered, laughing, did this ever happen? You know Frankie I want to give you a deep apology. What kind of man tries to shoot his dog, then shoot himself? A very sad despondent man with no hopes or dreams that who. You might say why not kill yourself, you Bill, and let me live but Frankie depression is a twisted world. You see Frankie no one ever believed in me, never gave me credit for anything. I worked hard to be the best, but my parents beat me down, took advantage of me when I was young.

I worked hard in school, I was the best as a rigger in the forest, you see Frankie I had talent and drive, but my dreams were beaten out of me, by forces I couldn't control.

Dreams Frankie, we own our history, this cannot be taken from us. We can also have dreams, but they hang on the slimmest of threads. "After I shot the white wolf", here Bill rubbed the spot on his head where even now the hair didn't grow back from the furrowing bullet, and most likely never would, "after the wolf and we walked out and left home, why Frankie I could begin to dream a little again". Here he shook his head, tears in his eyes and looked at me and said,

"Where am I Frankie?" And then he laughed like I hadn't seen him laugh ever.

He picked me up and let me lick his cheek, then while he put both of my paws on separate spokes of the great ships wheel, he started to say something, then stopped.

"Frankie, here is a little something just for you. This is a poem about Alaska, where we are headed. Think about it Frankie. Alaska, we are going to Alaska." Talk about dreams, I always wanted to go to Alaska.

Then in a deep voice, he started to recite:

"There are strange things done in the midnight sun
By the men who moil for gold.
The arctic trails have their secret tales
That would make your blood run cold.
The northern lights have seen queer sights,
But the queerest they ever did see,
Was that night on the marge of Lake Le Barge
I cremated Sam McGee."

"I won a prize in junior high school for reciting that poem, Franke."

Bill picked me up off of the dash by the compass and sat me on the chart table cushions.

I heard him say to himself, "Cattle Point on port. Frankie, there isn't a boat out tonight except us. We just passed Cattle Point light, that's a single flashing white light, port side, chart says Griffen Bay."

Slowly, cautiously we found our way at slow idle around Brown Island, coming face to face with the lights of Friday Harbor, San Juan Island, Washington State. The water was oily at night, with many lights of the village reflected and dancing on its polished surface. The scene was deserted, light rain circles tattooed the quiet inner harbor.

At dead slow in the dark, the twin cats barely rolling over, throatily rumbling, the large twin screws created quiet sucking sounds in our wake.

Bill saw the large dimly lighted sign.

"That's where we tie up for the night, Frankie, New England Fish Co., San Juan

Island, Washington State."

I could see the lighted main street of the village, heading up a hill behind the cannery, it was deserted, shops closed except one bar where its sign flashed red, on and off, Gertie's, open.

Bill had tried to rouse the crew for docking, but to no avail. They were drunk and still passed out. Bill thought to himself, I can do this better without a bunch of drunks stumbling and maybe falling over the side, especially in their condition.

So in preparation for docking the 86 footer, Bill laid out the large manilla lines on the gunnels, bow and stern. He laid out the lines for landing alone. The running loop of the line draped across the gunnel while the rest of the line was laid in orderly rows along the deck just inside the gunnel.

Looking down at me lying on the chart table's green cushions, Bill said, "I can rig a two hundred foot tree, climbing with my spurs, hang out in the wind and any kind of weather like a spider on a thin nylon web, the tree top whipping like mad, but God damn, landing a boat by myself in the middle of the night scares me to death."

He remembered advice from his father, "If the going gets rough, you can always go slower."

He couldn't go slower, he was at dead idle already. At dead idle, without thrust from the screws, a boat is as good as adrift on what ever current is flowing along side her hull.

Bill slid down the dark wheelhouse windows for better visibility light, cool mist flowed into the wheelhouse, he next opened the wheelhouse doors, port and starboard, and latched them. He looked aft and forward, in fact looked everywhere. We ghosted, dead slow, along side the cannery dock, finally creeping in and up to the old worn salmon scale encrusted ships dock. Small cranes, stood in the dark with booms and ropes, it all smelled like fish and creosote.

Bill shifted the engines into neutral and, with a providential tide and good luck, the Lynch sucked up against the dock, hanging there.

Bill ran down from the wheelhouse and reached out, putting a large loop of line over a great galvanized cleat from the bow, then ran alongside the gunnel and did the same on the stern, fastening her home, fore and aft, then he connected two spring lines. Going into the wheelhouse, he switched on the anchor light. Then he shut down the engines, one at a time. The bilge alarm sounded. He shut it off.

Bill was made for this life. He was good, even if he was a logger. Point of fact Bill was good at whatever he tried, however in his miserable life he just hadn't been given many chances. Bill hadn't been given a life of ease. It's curious in this life of our, dogs included, that some are just gifted and given the chance, there's the caveat given there chance, they begin growing like a weeds. But sad to say many are never given a chance, but this wasn't Bill's recent experience nor mine.

Stepping off onto the dock he connected us to the shore power. Looking back, he picked me off of the gunnel and set me on the old creosote and fish smelling dock. I could hear water sloshing, purling beneath the pier.

The dock and cannery seemed to my nose, deserted in the night, no one around. But remember even to dogs, scent is determined by upwind and down.

I made a run for a black dark rat that raced by me so closely that he made me jump. I could smell him. He smelled like garbage.

I barked and lunged at him, but missed. You probably know this if you know anything about Bichon's, but in our home country we are known as bringers of doom to rats.

As I sniffed around for the rat, Bill stood looking back at the sadly dilapidated old Cape Lynch huddled against the dock, listing 12 degrees, her deck load haphazard, some of the cargo had shifted even on the short passage from Seattle to Friday Harbor as we had rolled gently in the wake of a passing freighter.

The lines were neatly coiled on the deck where Bill had coiled them, while everything the crew did was askew.

When Bill was logging, he kept his saws razor sharp, cleaned and oiled, all of his gear was in top shape. Topping a one hundred and fifty foot redwood on the top of a stoney mountain, defying gravity, you don't get a second chance.

Bill mumbled to himself, "And I don't imagine you get too many second chances at sea either."

On all of the marine charts one could see little icons of sinking ships up and down the Pacific West Coast, indicative of the dangers of this lethal ocean.

The ocean is a gorilla that will kill you without emotion. To keep that from happening, check everything twice, and once more.

Luck's a chance, that means 50-50. As was said, "Luck's a chance, and trouble is sure."

"My experience," Bill told me, "was more like 60-40, 60 being against."

The fenders had been dragging since the disastrous departure from Fisherman's Wharf. Fisherman are a superstitious bunch, and dragging fenders was a bad sign.

The galley was cold, stove out, heavy snoring from the staterooms.

Bill thought to himself, "What a mess. The cook doesn't cook, worse he doesn't know how to cook, the engineer doesn't engineer, the skipper is a drunk taxi cab driver the rest of the year, and me? I'm a logger."

With this motley crew we are heading into some of the planet's most hellish seas.

The inside passage is really somewhat of a misnomer. Yes, part of the inside passage is sheltered, however, where we were headed it was turbulent, unpredictable, and help, in many places, well it didn't exist. When you broke down people would and could most often help, but the dark North Pacific is a very unforgiving place, and your boat out of power was then out of light, out of "way-on." Important to mention also, that there were very few other boats out there to assist in an emergency.

Your boat, no matter how large it was, was still a very minor blip on the surface of the dark and rolling old ocean. Reasoned preparation in every aspect, is key to survival at sea.

The inside passage to Alaska was wide open to the the vast North Pacific in multiple places. The wise mariner checked the tides and the local weather before attempting to cross these critical sea-exposed openings to the ocean.

While standing there looking around on the dark pier, light rain falling, an ancient mariner, salt encrusted, unshaven, limping as he walked, stepped out of the gloom from between two stacks of pallets beside a tall weathered red warehouse on the other side of the dock with New England Fish Co. painted in large chipped white letters.

Walking across over to us with a slight moan he said, "Would you happen to have a smoke?" He looked old and in decline, decaying, and to my fine sense of smell, finished with this life.

Bill shook him out a Lucky, then cupped his hands around the arthritic hands of the old fellow and while holding a stick match to the cigarette the old guy puffed it to light. The end of the cigarette glowed orange in the rain-dark.

The old fellow looked straight up into the misty dark sky, took a long drag on the Lucky, then coughed, spit, and coughed some more.

Then, kind of gagging on the cigarette, gasping out through watery eyes he said, "God damn that taste good, thanks."

Looking across the dock at the listing Cape Lynch he croaked out, "Who the hell loaded that boat, or are you leaking with that list?"

Bill off handedly said it was loaded by a ship of foolish drunks.

Well the old guy said, "I hope Friday Harbor is as far as you're going with that contraption loaded the way it is. Ya see, when you load a vessel so she lists 10-15 degrees when she is in rollers at sea, another 10-15 degree roller and you're at 20-30 degrees. Ya flip over quick like." It's pretty simple and mechanical the way that can happen, rolling over I mean, when you are not loaded right, same thing with death at the moment you roll, simple and mechanical.

Bill said, "We are heading far north of here in fact , we are bound away for Prince William Sound, up someplace in Alaska out across the gulf."

The old man shook his head sadly and said, "Is your life insurance paid up, Son? Because you will never make it loaded like that. Let me tell you something," he gasped out after a drag on the Lucky and a tissue tearing cough. "Where you're headed is not a school yard, not a place for the inexperienced, there's a lot to learn before heading where you are a-goin."

He took another pull on the Lucky and blew the smoke right into Bill's face. Bill was holding me and stepped back, the old man's fetid breath smelled revolting like vomit, and now also cigarettes.

Then he angrily shouted, little bits of spittle flying from his toothless mouth, "Listen to me carefully, God damn it, son, like your life depends on it, because it does. The Inside is not a cozy, friendly cruise north. It's a hellish, wind moaning, rock strewn passage with more twists and turns than your small bowel. The Inside passage has a protected sound to it don't it, but don't let it fool ya. It ain't protected in many places, and even where it is protected it can be a wind tunnel with typhoon forces. Waves build up in those small places like short solid rock walls, and it's always worse at night.

"Play only by the rules of the sea. Your own personal erratic rules out there don't matter. Have a good engine mechanic who is also an electrician, a top notch skipper, up to date charts, a tuned compass, two radars, and a good boat, with this arrangement you will be fine."

Then he winked and said, "Most of the time your crew, your boat and preparation is the foundation to survival. The inside north from Seattle is lined with sunken ships, the ghostly cries of dead seaman, solid rusting engines lie on the bottom that will never run again.

"I have 130 trips across Queen Charlotte Sound. Oh yeah, God damn it, too much booze, I forgot. I have 129 and one half trips, the last one we got only half way across. I will tell you about that in a moment.

"They call Queen Charlotte Sound, the 'killing fields,' the name should explain it. The bottom is plated with sunken ships, the boats crewed and captained by the dead.

"Go outside in the open ocean off the west coast of Vancouver Island, heading north to try to avoid the inside, well forget that, there are more sunken ships out there than inside if possible! Fisherman that would give their lives to moil for dollars think of nothing but treasure with no consequences for their reckless actions.

They throw seabags over their shoulders, leaving crying children, angry wives, creditors, friends, and home to fish in whatever kind of weather the sea offers. The sea offers up its potion, and we sailers have no choice except to take the shaky spoonfuls of Neptunes potion he holds up to our lips and dance the Danse Macabre. And will there be fish?, always the sixty-four thousand dollar question. But you can bet on this when there is a plethora of fish, the price will be down, when there are no or few fish, the price will be up. It's not a game for the faint of heart or the dumb and or inexperienced.

"I know, I am one of those sorry sons-a-bitches that danced. As soon as the moorings are cast off, your danger begins, even from the west wall to the Ballard Locks, danger is everywhere on the water, inside and out. Funny about life on the sea, the harder you work the further your dream keeps receding. Some make a small pile, but most cash in for wages if they are lucky, and others with their lives if Neptune is in a bad mood. And their loved ones on the beach? They weep.

"For the loss of a nail, the horse is lost, for the loss of the horse, the King is lost, for the loss of the King, the castle is lost.

"To extend that analogy," he said, "a boat at sea is a boat load of nails. Anything that can go wrong will go wrong.

It can be as simple as a small innocent brass screw that holds the steerage assembly that comes undone some where in the dim-dark bowels of the boat. All of a sudden you can't steer the boat. On the inside passage, in many places there is very little room to maneuver in an emergency. Perhaps a simple 50 cent gasket on a carburetor comes loose, the engine starts sucking air in the middle of a storm in the North Pacific. Nothing like being without power, rolling sideways back and forth in the trough, back and forth and back again, in a sloppy confused swell.

Or perhaps you are on your back, under a gigantic cold engine, an oily pillow beneath your head, trying to find and fix a devastating problem in an oily bilge under this unresponsive monster engine. This destroys your composure. Boats are made to take seas head on, not roll back and forth until you are beaten black and blue. This is a dangling modifier in the oceans book of knowledge.

"Try fishing your oil-blackened hand in a foot and a half of oily bilge under a D17000 caterpillar engine for a vital 3/4 inch socket. Oil covering your arm up past your elbow and then some. Either find that socket or perhaps drift onto rocks and die. So simple, so elemental, so dire."

Finally, standing there in the foggy mists and rains the old fisherman, the decaying old fisherman croaked out this tale, he told us of a horrifying event in his own life in the spring of 1948.

"He took a drag on the lucky, then he coughed, then he spit a greenish white splat on the dock and began his story:

You may know that 1948 in Alaska was a year of disastrous fishing. Many lost their boats, the fish just didn't come. You may be aware that when something is rare, men take added chances and risks, to achieve what is sometimes impossible, no matter how risky or how hard they try events swing out of their reach.

Well we were on the Aldebaran, an old Alaska limit seiner, 58 feet, a boat type that was built in Hoonah, Alaska sometime before God. She's of course gone now. She was pretty in her youth, the Aldebaran. She was stout, Port Orford cedar beneath the waterline and straight vertical grain spruce above with steamed oak ribs. She had a heavy duty Washington diesel electric. When she was built she was top notch. She had a white hull and red lead beneath the waterline. She was a beauty, but somehow unsuccessful. Funny how some boats even with good skippers, though this is more rare, but some boats for what ever reason, don't attract fish.

Then there are the poor and neglectful owners, lack of up keep, and the relenting rigors of the sea that eventually destroy any good boat.

Have you ever seen a drop dead gorgeous woman with the wrong man? He leads her astray until her makeup is pasty and runs, she dresses wrong, he gets her to smoke until she coughs all the time, her teeth become loose and rotten, her breath smells, her joints creak and crack, her digestion is flatulent. Boat, woman, all the same.

The Aldebaran was sunk once by carelessness, then raised, refitted with a more modern diesel, then someone put one of the God awful southeastern flying bridge houses on her, which was lipstick on a pig. She became a parody of herself. Rust ran down the once white hull, her anchor dripped rust down her bow, she listed with the flying bridge, she was a beauty far down on her luck, with a fouled seaweed and barnacled bottom. An old beauty queen with no makeup. Boat, woman, all the same. Take care of your women, men, and take special care of your boat, it is your body on the ocean's deep.

"No one wanted to sail on the Aldebaran in her aged condition: old, slow, old, rotten, old, dangerous, think drowning.

"Got an another cigarette?" he said hopefully. "And I'll tell you a story that will make your blood run cold."

As he cupped the match in the waining light I could see his quivering jaw muscles, his neck ligaments, tighter than the rat lines on the Cape Lynch, his drooping weathered eyes, his loose, pliable flesh weighing down his lips.

The geologic wrinkles in his old crumbling face were a worn, decaying headland with dead silvered whiskers for trees. He probably wondered how old he was.

His eyes were mere geologic fissures, cracks in his face. In the instant of the match's sulfurous flare, his slouched wet dark wool hat pulled low, it seemed his whole conglomerate life's history was revealed in his ravaged, storm tattered physiognomy. One could see in that face the brutal gouging sea born gales, hear the salted screams of the gulls, understand his blistered, sun ravaged skin, feel the rise on towering North Pacific swells, see the weight on his shoulders of the God thing called the sea. We could imagine him vomiting in cheap heads on Creek Street in Ketchikan. His history was his future. It was spooky, and it sure wasn't pretty. A sack of guts in pickled flesh.

He opened his bearded, mustached, slack mouth, a Lucky once again hanging from one side. Then out from the black cave of his mouth, out to the ends of undiscovered time, over meerschaum colored rotted teeth, came a rasping voice, heavy, ponderous with personal grief and continual abuse, plus a hell of a lot of experience that he probably would have been a hell of a lot better off for not knowing, however such was not his case. His life rode him hard and put him away wet, and life that innocent thing, was constantly crushing him. He knew this, but where oh where to run in his limited world? Everyone seemed to have something and he had nothing, not even a dog.

He began speaking, croaking with this unusual archival voice, thinking slowly, finding so painfully scrunching up his eyes to make his thought clearer, way back, searching his way through, and passed his tongue, far back into his alcohol infused brain to that early spring in the year 1948.

He found his way past too many bars and too many double shots of Jack cemented in his bones like a conglomeration of pre-science ghosts. Past thick bloody rib-eyed steaks, more whiskey and torment. Crawling down rain soaked deserted late night docks in Klawock, Sitka, Kodiak, Hoonah, anywhere there was a drink. Sometimes following a Klooch, more often alone.

"Here," he would say, standing in some bar while fishing his stinking fish slimed saline crumpled money out of his pocket.

"Here," he would say, holding his wad of money high for the waitress while at the same time, pulling out, his bull Durham pouch, rolling another cancer nail, cough, gag, then when the waitress came, order a triple round for every one in the dilapidated joint. He was a fisherman, he knew how

it was done. Death before dishonor, the seaman's creed.

Here Bill and I wondering what would
come next, listening in awe, watching as
he searched his febrile feverish mind like
a boat's searchlight in thick fog. We could
see in the crags and rivers of his riven face
this searching in the tangled folds of his
thoughts, past the bars, past the divorces,
past the abandonments, peering here and
there for that fresh spring 1948 morning far
back in the recesses of his distant thoughts,
up somewhere on Queen Charlotte Sound's
vastness.

"Certain experiences stay in your
mind," he said, "like bullets over your head
in a battle. You don't forget."

He pulled a blackened stub of a cigarette out of his shirt pocket, held it up to
his moist mouth while Bill struck another
wooden match and lit it for him.

"So it was like this," he started to choke,

then inhaled sharply, then sobbed. Tears found the estuarial channels in his riverine face.

"Well, anyway," he said, as he got control of his emotions, gathering himself. "That morning we were creeping up the inside, several days out of Seattle. I remember we were north of Alert Bay, approaching Hope Island at the north entrance to Queen Charlotte Sound. As I now recall, it's been so many years, it was a blue sky day. Deceiving, considering what happened. If you don't know where Hope Island is, it's on the north east corner of Vancouver Island.

"All that morning the sea was restless, rough in its bed. Funny the sea, like a personalty. Ever been with a friend where you can tell they are riled? Well we angled up, passing through Broughton Channel and, as I said, we took Alert Bay on our starboard. The sea without white caps was vibrating, rolling even inside under the low cover of hope Island west of Goleta channel. Clinging to Nigel Island's western shore we finally made a break out at the northern tip of Hope island and Bull harbor, making our run heading for Fitz Hugh Sound, across Queen Charlotte Sound. It's a long run across Queen Charlotte Sound, we had some of the crew sleeping, and the rest of us were in the galley playing cribbage, the boat was on auto pilot aimed for the distant Cape Calvert and the entrance to Fitz Hugh sound and back into potentially quieter water. Light patches of sea fog filled in the sea here and there, while above was blue sky and sun. Playing cribbage and laughing and shouting we were all brought to our feet by the loud strident blasting of a ships horn very near by. All of us ran to the bridge just in time to see us pass between a large sea-going tug in front of us and it's gargantous barge behind us, and the cable between the barge and the tug running beneath our boat. We escaped certain death by seconds. Fishermen are a superstitious bunch and this event shook us to the core. There was darkness and carelessness in this and Neptune doesn't suffer fools, the innocents maybe, but the fools, rarely.

"Local weather channels gave no unusual indication of poor weather, though the barometer, another adjective or verb for your information, was dropping." He stopped talking for a moment then shouted, "Remember this, God damn it, all weather is local! Well, it was like this, the further we pushed out into Queen Charlotte Sound the sea turned from long soft insistent large rollers to freakish terrifying green smooth towering mountains of sunlit emerald sea water. These rollers slapped against the port side of the Aldebaran out of the west, and washed the decks with foaming white salty sea.

"The further we edged out into Queen

Charlotte Sound the steeper and more numerous the waves became, in a word, another word in your book of the sea, the frequency of the vibrations of the wave changed to dramatically shorter intervals. The strange, even scary part was the waves didn't break, but continued to swell, still surging mightily, smoothly, higher and higher. Boats traveling near us would disappear in the bottom of these gigantic smooth swells, then they would rise, silhouetting against the sky, then disappear, again and again and again.

"At the top of each swell, we seemed to freeze in this teeter-totter place where we hung, all of the Aldebaran's massive, water logged old bulk defying gravity. Then like a guillotine the bow dropped. The stern shot high into the saline-blue sky. It rose over the sinking bow, the screw caveating, then the bow plunged into the greasy sea like a diving whale.

"'Jesus!' yelled Louie, our now dead skipper, as the on coming waves buried Aldebaran's bow, 'Come up, God damn it, come up!

Get your life jackets on boys!'

"It seemed to each of us as the bow plummeted, leading the stern down like flukes on a whale, that it was all over, and little did we know, it was.

"Finally, ponderously shuddering and shaking like a wet rusty white dog with a white bone in its teeth, cracking and moaning, the old antique Aldebaran stopped her decent as the screws finally found solid sea water to bite into, driving the hesitating Aldebaran back to the surface. As we arose, endless tons of white foaming seawater poured off her bows and stern.

"Finally rising yet again, we hit that balance point where the decks were sun lit and glistening wet. Then, with the antique hull complaining, creaking, moaning, once again rose on the next wave, the bow plunged, and then the whole nektonic nightmare began again, then again. Queen Charlotte Sound is an illusionist. She can look passive, don't buy it boys, for in reality, she is a killer.

"Remember," here he looked meaningfully right into Bill's youthful blue eyes, "the sea has no conscience. If you die, it isn't because the sea tried to kill you, it was that you were in the wrong place at the wrong time, and unprepared to find yourself in that place, nothing personal."

A raggedy young kid that had joined us from a fish boat nearby on the dark fog enshrouded dock asked the old fellow, "What happens if your engine quits, your air starts are empty, while you are drifting on the weather shore toward the rocks?"

The old man chuckled like a crackling voice from a coffin and said, "Son, you don't get in that position. The experienced mariner checks the tides, the weather, fastens his loads again, plans, and yet fastens them once more. Checks and rechecks his charts, mountainous rocky peaks can lie under a foot of water. Assassins, killers Son, are everywhere beneath the sea. And you can remember this my young friend, if you fall over and drown some creature beneath the waves will be very very happy, every scrap of you will be eaten and enjoyed, even fought over.

"Alone on the Pacific is like you have never been alone before. To be adrift on these rock strewn shores is a death sentence.

"These gabbling, muttering shores are filled with new and old death and destruction. There are rusted, decayed, rotted, sunken wrecks everywhere. Plan carefully.

To be dead for a second is to be dead for eternity.

There are few second chances in the games the sea plays. She holds all the cards.

"Perhaps a curious seal, a diving duck, maybe a sleek otter, a halibut may know where your boat went down, but for sure your boat will never return to the fleet, ever. Never again will your boat be bright with new paint, bright brass polished railings, new nets, loaded with food and stuffs of the living. Never again with gear and vitality will you be 'faring out on the wild and open old ocean, searching for the silver darlings,' on the oh so pretty, gentle, dangerous, sun-lit swells.

"Nor will the crews who so bravely, with such confidence, set out for riches. There will be no welcome home. The crews will be asleep with the fish they sought, the tables turned, the fisherman becomes fish food. Rather than powering on up the inside, engines at full throttle to the fishing grounds, instead they will be there on the sub oceanic sea bed. Their boat, now lost forever, will sit on the bottom, the playground of motes of wavering sunlight in the rocky shadowed shallows. The empty watery engine room filled with fish, octopus, motes of life, the bunks and staterooms dead yet alive, and from the wheelhouse, a compass pointing somewhere, the ships wheel frozen in place, the iron mike silent for once.

Those mariners that are unlucky or don't plan become a playground for the ebbing and flooding currents of the sea, their ghost-like bodies abraded forwards and backwards until they are no more. There will be innocent crabs, small simple colorful fish, little nektonic creatures, not bigger than the head of a pin, that will play in the eroded seaman's skull, while the sea continuously, geologically fills in the drowned seaman's briny dreams of riches with sandy detritus.

"'How do you figure that into the price of a pound of fish," the old man fairly shouted.

The old seaman, tears flowing, continued, "Our whole crew stood riveted in the wheelhouse, which now had about six inches of sea water sloshing back and forth, watching as we listed this way then that, horror at each mast high wave that swept beneath us. As we continued on across Queen Charlotte Sound toward the aptly named Cape Caution off to our starboard, the weather began to change, the waves began by breaking, slamming against us harder and much for the worse rising up to the galley windows before subsiding only to rise again and again.

"Finally we noticed small light cats paws on the smooth high rolling greased seas. Little white ruffles, then larger ruffles, then finally waves breaking over each other as though they were in a rush to consummate our destruction. These waves started to break at the same time the height of the rollers dramatically increased. Each wave, a white bone in its mouth, broke over on it-self. The light wind, which had been calm for the entire day, switched from the south to hard driving off our port side directly out of the turbulent western Gulf of Alaska.

"The winds boys, the winds," the old guy said, "are fickle like some women." Then he laughed.

"Once, one night dancing with a beau-tiful Aleut woman in the Cordova House bar- oh hell, I will tell you that story anoth-er time," he said as he wiped tears, both humorous and intensely sad, from his fur-rowed eyes.

Meanwhile, as he was talking, Smitty sheepishly, leadenly, slowly stepped over the gunnel and out onto the dock, listening to the old guy's tale. The aged seaman was quiet for a while, then looking at Smitty with a glimmer of hope in his crusty eyes, ever so gently asked Smitty if perchance he had, he said this very cautiously, ever so gently he asked if perhaps, Smitty had a drink on board for an old fellow salt.

Smitty with out a word, quietly reached over under the gunnel where a bottle of Jack Daniels had lodged after our drunken departure from Seattle, handed it to the old fellow and said, "It's yours." It was full, un-opened.

The old guy lit up, rubbed his mouth up and down with the palm of his hand, rotated the cap, threw it over his shoulder, and thirstily guzzled a long pull until a third of the bottle's whiskey had disappeared down his stale, weather-scared throat. I've seen wolves greedily eat and drink like he did. I could see the Jack going down his throat, his Adam's apple bobbing.

"Well," the grizzled antique then said, "the weather increased along with our fears on the peak of every mountainous wave. We had no choice, we couldn't turn back. To turn broad side to those waves was certain suicide, besides by this time our deck cargo had shifted and we were listing ten degrees, we would roll for sure, heavily loaded as we were and listing if we had tried to go about."

He looked at the kid and said, "Sometimes, Kid, the only option is to continue, remember that. Right or wrong, lucks a choice and a chance.

"Well," he continued, "as we drove into the dark, Cape Caution rose on our starboard just after dusk, just where it should be, flashing its steady 120 flashes per minute, warning the mariner of the extreme danger existing there. Deadly as the glistening eyes of a viper, it flashed its warning.

"Darkness came on, bleary in the salt washed wheelhouse windows, and as it often does at dark, the weather quickly changed. The western wind dramatically rose from a relatively calm Beaufort 4-5 to a tempestuous Beaufort 9-10. I may not look like much to you men, but once I was an English teacher. I don't suppose you have ever heard the poem 'O Western Wind When Wilt Thou Blow?'

"'The small rain down can rain. Christ! My love were in my arms and I in my bed again.' Well lads, we all wished we were home and in bed in our loves arms, not on this terrible sea.

"The waves hissed by, rising even, the were continually slopping over the tops of our gunnels, our flags were whipping, shredding. As we turned on our deck lights we saw the sea was frothy, filled with fury, angry, threatening." The hissing winds cried die.

The old seaman took another hit off the bottle and looking again sideways at the kid, and said, "We are so small compared to the sea. Remember," he said, "there is nothing vengeful in the sea. We were in the wrong place at the wrong time, but sometimes in this life there is no warning. When you are falling you fall and figure out what happened to you when you try to rise.

"The massive waves continued to build.

On every wave the Aldebaran rose, shuddering, cavitating, shaking. Glasses and plates were falling out of the wall racks, stools fell over in the wheelhouse, what wasn't tied down slid. The top heavy southeastern flying bridge house carried us, listing further over on each swell like a clock's pendulum. Some things, our port life boat for one, who knew what else or when, washed overboard into the now furious green and white lathered tumult.

"Rounding Cape Caution three miles out, we saw the Cape Calvert light at the entrance to Fitz Hugh sound flashing in the far distance off our port bow. We would never make it that far. Rain, predictable with the vastly increasing winds, now started beating like gravel against our windows.

This was no place for sissies, and especially green horns. Remember this when you set out in that scow across the dock tomorrow.

Rising on one gigantic comber, the tired decaying hull teeter tottered in the air. Her screw uselessly thrashing air, the bow without direction from her airborne rudder, the whole boat shaking, shuddering, plates falling, engine room smoking, decks glistening.

"Just at that exact moment a plank of aged Port Orford yellow cedar, an old hull plank held on for years by water pressure and rusted nail fasteners, popped and sprung. The plank dropped into the sea, leaving a fissure ten inches wide, fourteen feet long. She was opened with a devastating lethal gash. A scalpel like slash, a wound to her guts, sliced so cleanly a surgeon couldn't have sliced her so expertly, everything inside instantly exposed, no redemption. We filled with icy sea water in nano seconds. An inch and a half of yellow cedar, ten inches wide, fourteen feet long, between us and our maker, gone, just a icy watery hell staring at us from the lockers of Neptune.

"The heavy winds with Beaufort scale of 9-11, seas from the open Pacific slashed and hammered our port side. As she quickly filled we rolled, snap your fingers, that quick. We are so small, we who sail the sea in ships, the sea so vast. We were over on our starboard side in seconds, then completely upside down in the blink of an eye. Listen to me you green horns, God damn it, in a blink.

"So quick, you just can't imagine how fast death comes at sea, the sea with no angry intent. Remember, the sea is neither good nor evil, it just is. No years and months of sickness leading to death, no long miserable stays and dying in hospitals, no previous moment of thought that the end was near.

No warnings. A pain in the side, a faulty heart valve, no nothing like that. Aldebaran, veteran of the seas, slid beneath the sea, bow down, upside down, and down, without a sobbing whimper.

"Maybe some fish could hear some muted breaking things falling inside, perhaps the great engine, pulled her bolts and fell. Who knows, maybe the fish heard something, who knows what a fish hears. So soon, so quick, so fast the screw was still turning, until the icy North Pacific filled her exhaust stacks, choking the last life from the old Washington diesel electric, its giant pistons still pumping, then nothing remained on the surface where we had been, gone, gone, gone," he wept.

"Did you shout out for help?" the kid said.

He looked over at the kid with tears and said, "Hardly had time to shout, but shout to who in the black, wind driven coast, where not a light was to be seen? Cape Caution was still warning mariners at 120 flashes a minute, and where we had once been, now nothing. Some flotsam and jetsam and a few bubbles from drowning men, and nothing else.

"Salvation? No, no salvation. Mouthfuls and lungs filling with sea water as we rolled over. I caught the faintest glimpse of the Cape Calvert light, then frigid dark. In mere moments the sea filled in and we were gone."

Here more tears filled his cleft, grief-filled face. Putting one arthritic hand over his eyes, he blindly reached out with his other quivering hand, toward Smitty who put the bottle of Jack in his hands. Gathering himself after a long, shuttering, throat ripping sound, he took a gigantic gulp, too big a gulp, he choked. Then gagging on the Jack, he spit it out in a yellow whiskey splat on the dock, laboring to breath. He was drowning in whiskey.

He then took a long draining slug, finally emotionally gasping out, "They all died. Died, you understand? They never had nor took it under consideration that life could be here, then it wasn't. Their lives ended at that moment for each of them, all of them."

"Were you scared?" the kid said.

"Fear? Jesus, hell no. No one had time to be frightened. Were you frightened when you were born? Well they all died the same way, gagging, not on their mother's birthing fluids, rather on the seawater of our Earth Mother. They were equally unafraid, birth and death, same entrance, same exit."

Then he laughed and coughed, then cried, "Oh blessed Jesus! She ponderously, quickly, with intent, rolled over on her starboard. In the scary dark wheelhouse we all fell, as the icy seas broke windows, filled and poured down the stack, then finally throttled the Aldebaran. Next we knew we were standing on the wheelhouse ceiling. The hull filled, every last small pocket, then the ocean, the great, ill-named Pacific Ocean filled the lung sacks of our drowning crew. Reaching, gasping, eyes wide, no God, no devil, just the passive ocean, close and personal at the moment of their distress."

Bill looked at the Lynch as the old seaman, head in hand, cried. The Lynch, disheveled, old, falling apart, a crew that couldn't sail, none were seamen, none familiar, none that knew the inside passage north, none that had a relationship with the sea. What the hell?

Bill turned, looking at Smitty. He was hung over, his face looked like a grey landslide, then over at the old seaman, watching as he had turned while he staggered up the dock, sobbing.

As we watched him go, he suddenly turned around from far up the cold, dark, rain driven dock and pulled his old yellow seaman's Sou'Wester hat off his balding head. The sickly yellow dock lights gave him a stark meanness.

He looked back with hatred, disbelief, toward us where we were still standing, shocked by his tale on the creosoted dock by the Lynch, and in a maniacal, angry, screaming voice, his eyes evil and grotesque, shouted, "Plan ahead! Wear your God damn life jackets. That's why I lived and they didn't. Do you understand? The sea plays no games that a solitary man can possibly understand! When it's you and the sea you, God damn it, have to think a lot. The sea doesn't give a damn if you live or die, so you better think. Be prepared and if your aren't, prepare for death.

"And one more thing, you rag tag looking bunch misfits. You will never make it even to Campbell River with your boat loaded like that. The men, seaman, still alive that

I knew, worked hard, studied hard, learned from good men, listened, paid attention, and the rest? They are dead, drowned. I see them too often in my nightmares. Lifeless eyes, putrid bodies rolling back and forth on the bottom of the sea, where crabs and small fish feed on them."

We all started to turn to board the Lynch and get out of the rain when the antique sea-man turned and walked back up the dock toward us. We stopped, waiting expectant-ly. Coming drunkenly before us he stood there a moment, weaving back and forth like sea reeds in light airs.

Then out of his mouth came a desperate angry explosion of a shout, "Listen, damn you! When we seamen go to sea, we stand at every point at each moment before a judge. These moments at points and capes, storms and darkness, they are all interviews with higher mighty forces. Will you be up to it? From what I see of you dilapidated misfits,

I think NOT!" he shouted. "We may think we are. We think, 'Oh sure, we are all set. We are lashed, secure, tied down, ready to meet the sea. We have got it figured out. No problem,' we think. But remember you need to lash down your thinking, most importantly.

"Listen, life is decided for us quickly. You may think you are in control, but you are not. Forces on grand trajectories are in charge. Shit, you dumb bastards, you struggled just getting to Friday Harbor from Seattle. Any simple weekend sailor can do that."

He turned suddenly, starting to choke up again, nearly fell, then quietly, shaking his fist at us in the wet dark fog, spit, took another pull on the Jack, turned, and disappeared, a dirty grey ghostly spectral walking out of our lives into the salted rain and fog. The last thing I saw was the dim orange glow of his cigarette. The last thing I heard was the splash of the empty Jack bottle as it took an air burial into the Salish Sea.

Bill was clearly shaken. He turned to Smitty, saying with emotion, "Frankie and I are done. We have no desire to leave our bones strewed on the seafloor between here and anywhere. Goodnight."

Smitty caught him by the sleeve and passionately said, "Can we please talk in the morning, Bill?"

"Good night, Smitty. I'm up early and gone," Bill said.

Earlier the next morning while Bill and Smitty quietly talked, I lay sleeping in a dry place under the wide gunnel on the black creosoted deck, one brown eye open, watching Bill's face. I could always tell his mood just by looking at his eyes. We dogs are like that.

This morning I couldn't tell what was what. Finally I saw them shake hands. Smitty had a big smile. You know we dogs show our teeth when we are angry. Smitty was showing his, however he was very happy, not angry.

We spent the morning and most of the rest of the day reloading and rearranging the load.

Bill tied and retied the ponderous deck load until he shouted up at Smitty, who was leaning out the wheelhouse window smoking, and said, "Okay, we are secure as we can get."

It was getting dark when Smitty shouted down into the galley and told Trigve to fire up the twin cats. Throwing off the lines, we backed out into the channel, port screw in idle forward, starboard screw idle speed in reverse. We turned in our length. Slowly we made our way up out of Friday Harbor in the fresh salt night air and on up Trincomali Channel on the east side of the Gulf Islands. I stood on the bow, my ears waving, smelling the loamy dirt from the land and, as always, the over powering richness of the sea. Lights from small cabins and buoys and the occasional passing boat quavered on the still waters.

Thanks to Bill, the Cape Lynch was trimmed, balanced, and shipshape. Some people just know how to do it. They seem born with it. They're good at whatever they touch.

OH CANADA

Coming up on Nanaimo, British Columbia on our port side, we broke out into the middle of the lower straits of Georgia, took a 90 degree course change to port, and continued our night time journey hugging the eastern Vancouver Island shore northbound.

The northern part of the strait was cluttered with all sizes of islands and gigantic boulders barely under water at certain tides. The whole of the strait was littered with ship wrecks.

On the sea bottom of the straits the winds and the tides and currents rolled the bare, crab-gnawed bones of the drowned dead.

At sea, as the old sorrowful seaman on the dock said last night, we were always on the edge of life and death.

We don't fight against the symptoms of the sea. The sea is a real, vibrating, living creature. Sailing on the sea is a constant fight against an eternal marine machine that grinds down stoney headlands and sinks ships like the Titanic. She can be calm as water in a glass or tempestuous as a pus plagued bubonic.

The sea can be soporific or a mind bending mystic, where and what you think you see isn't always the case, and this causes extreme anxiety. Anxiety can cause vast, disparate feelings. What you see might be there, and then maybe not. Misjudge you run aground, maybe die.

Passing Campbell River on the port, we headed up into Discovery Passage where the world famous Ripple Rock once existed. Ripple Rock was the site of one of the world's largest non-nuclear explosions. There once existed a gigantic underwater mountain that was responsible for the sinking of 119 ships before it was blown to smithereens in 1958. As we powered north passed this spot in Seymour narrows the tides still, even with the rock severely degraded still twisted and turned the old Cape Lynch in the powerful currents. Proceeding north we came to Chatham Point and took a sharp port turn into the vast slice of sea called Johnstone Strait. It's wind-driven rocky shores thrust northward to Queen Charlotte Strait, and then the devil's own hell in wild weather, Queen Charlotte Sound, with the wide open, poorly named Pacific Ocean on the port side.

This morning, after our six hour watch, Bill and I gratefully made ourselves a light breakfast and climbed into our bunk for a much needed rest. Our all night vigil at the wheel watch took it out of us. The cook was still sequestered in his stateroom.

Bill, with me at his feet, once opened the cook's door to try and get him to cook. When he opened the door the cook, with a cigarette in one hand and a bottle of whiskey in his other hand, stood in the middle of the room, pissing in a can. He yell at us to get the hell out of there. Bill quietly closed the door.

Night time on the sea is nothing like daytime. It is exhausting, fraught with blindness. Out there on the deep as darkness falls, fear and anxiety rise. Everywhere it seems there are lights, winking and flashing near and far. The far lights weakly flash and show themselves far off in the distant galaxy of the islands. Lighthouse lights flashing warnings from their glass Fresnel eyes, deadly as snakes. Lighted buoys, red and green lights, warn of death and destruction. The seaman must know his charts. To get off a light is as good as being off a mile, something like mistaking a red light for a green light at a highway intersection and not slowing down.

Ships near and far off in the darkness show red light for port side, green for starboard. A boat coming straight at you in the darkness will show red, port, green starboard, collision course. A boat passing by on your port side will also show a port red light, passing on the starboard, a green light, port to port, starboard to starboard. Obviously a boat heading straight at you in the dark where you can see both port and starboard lights means collision eminent. Five short blasts on your ship's horn means evasive action is necessary immediately by both vessels. Ostensibly, such as two cars on a highway, when head to head, one car goes right and the other car goes right, thereby avoiding a collision.

Coming up behind a slower vessel in the dark from the rear she will show a white stern light. The stern light must be visible from two nautical miles and project light backwards across the horizon in a 135 degree arc. The stern light can be combined with the masthead light to make up 360 degrees.

Beside ships, boats, and barges, there is the floating drift of all manner floating off the shores and down rivers into in the sea. There is everything from barrels and planks, to logs and roots, derelict boats, tires and unrooted buoys. The Dreaded log booms dimly lit by wand red lanterns, deadly as a water-logged island if you hit one. Shore lights of homes, distant low stars, all add to the confusion. The sea at night is a kaleidoscope of multicolored, tessellated warnings that must be seen and heeded or risk the ship, cargo and crew. To be oblivious to these warnings is gravely perilous. Throw into the mix novice boaters, drunk captains, men relying on their automatic pilot while they sleep, the perils are manifold.

The thing, luck, was with us crossing a glass smooth Queen Charlotte Sound. We passed Cape Caution on our starboard, entered Fitz Hugh Sound, passing Sorrow Islands and Grief Bay, and Calvert Light on our port. Continuing on we passed the old First Nations village of Bella Bella, Tolmie Channel, continuing north through Discovery Channel, then finally passing into the long running Grenville Channel. Grenville Channel is a slot of ocean bordered by snow capped mountains and rarely calm, with few hiding places.

This morning while passing Prince Rupert on our starboard, Bill told Smitty, who was on the wheel, that he and I were getting off the Cape Lynch in Ketchikan unless the useless cook got up and made us something to eat.

Smitty told Bill, "Take the wheel," and went below to rouse the cook.

In about thirty minutes the old cook shouted up to Smitty, "Chow is ready."

Rushing below, starving, we found the cook had taken a galvanized wash tub, put in a dozen heads of chopped up iceberg lettuce, and very liberally soaked it with thousand island dressing. That was it.

Bill said, "We're off in Ketchikan, screw this."

Luck was with us once more. We passed the highly dangerous Dixon entrance, finally coasting northward up Douglas Channel, passed by Saxman Totem Park on our starboard, and approached Ketchikan just as the evening lights were coming on. This long day, however, wasn't done with us.

We were all anxious to get off of the boat, so anxious that when Smitty came around out in Douglas channel to land to the south, putting the Lynch along side the steamer dock port side, he misjudged his speed and hit the dock square on our bow. What could we expect? Smitty was a taxi cab driver, not a fishing skipper. He was hired by a friend in the fishing office.

Bill fell onto the deck. Worse, our old cook, handling the stern line, fell off the boat into the jade green glacial water. I began to bark loudly, alerting everyone of man overboard. Very fortunately the engineer was on the stern and threw the old useless cook a life ring.

Once tied fore and aft, including spring lines, the massive D17000 horse power twin cats were shut down, grumbling, bilge alarms shut off, bilges checked, they were dry. In a word, we were shipshape. After re-securing our cargo in Friday Harbor, nothing had moved on our trip north to Ketchikan, thanks to Bill's expert talent and supervision.

Standing on the pier, Bill and I were getting used to our sea legs when Smitty walked up to us. After the cook episode he said he wanted to take us out to dinner. He said he had another friend, a skipper on the 58 footer the Cape Fear, a black steel purse seine fishing boat with a white house, tied nearby on an adjacent dock. The Cape Fear was also bound for Cordova.

Smitty said his friend Arne, the skipper of the Cape Fear, with his new Russian mail-order bride, were going to join us for drinks and dinner at the Ketchikan House. The venerable old bar that was hanging, defying gravity, over Creek Street. Creek Street was once the red-light district in old Ketchikan.

A number of the old timers with the right seining licenses started their fishing in Bristol Bay on the north side of the Aleutians, then fished Prince William Sound, then Southeastern Alaska, then continuing to follow the southward migrating silver river of fish, ending up fishing in Puget Sound.

The Cape Fear skipper was one of these briny, salt-cured men that followed the fish south each year. The whole North Pacific showed in his face. His new Russian bride, well she was something else. No English, just a doughy face, wolf blue eyes, and large, heavily coated red lips like red lead.

We left the boat in rain, fog, deepening darkness, clad in our yellow Helle-Hansen rain gear, rubber red dot boots and Sou'Wester hats. Bill carried me. The bar was packed tight as salmon in a trap. The windows were foggy with streams of water on their dripping surfaces. In one corner of the old smoked bar was a crude stunted stage. Sitting there with a red and chrome accordion, an old man was playing "Laura's Theme" from the movie Dr. Zhivago.

Bill didn't need to exercise himself

about bringing a dog into that bar. Seemed to me small, little white fellow that I am, that everywhere I looked there were some monstrous, wild looking wolf-dogs sleeping here and there all around the room.

Out on the dance floor an Indian woman, still in her cannery worker clothes, was dancing with a heavily bearded sad looking fisherman in a quarter of an inch of gin. They were, shall I be nice, impaired. They were twirling and twisting the way drunks do, amorous and smash-mouth kissing. The whole floor was crowded with a malodorous, jostling crowd. The accordionist had nine filled to the rim glasses of Jack lined up beside him as he played on. On the other side of his chair were five empty glasses and a plate that some dog was licking.

We followed Smitty to a crowded little table right by the dance floor. Here we met his friend Arne, skipper from the Cape Fear, and his Russian mail-order bride, Marina.

She was a bleached blond, pasty white face with dimples like fox holes in her cheeks, lip stick the color of old blood, dressed in tight fitting black leather clothes that looked like they were sprayed on.

She opened her bright red lips and said, "Zdrast vooytie," over rotted teeth.

Her husband, obviously admiring her, said while laughing, "That means hello in Russian. She's from Siberia."

She said something in Russian, which Arnie interpreted that she said from her Siberian village they could see Alaska.

Then they both reached down, tossing off double shots of fresh glasses of Stolichnaya vodka. She had a tight fitting black leather bomber jacket that barely contained her creamy breasts stuffed in between the silver zippers of her jacket.

We all sat down while Smitty ordered us, his crew, drinks and steaks. The drinks came immediately. Sitting quietly surveying this motley crew, Bill jumped, startled, when Arne's bride whirled off the dance floor and landed right on his lap with both of her fat little arms around Bill's neck, love at first sight. Arne, her husband, frowned at this action.

I watched from my place under the table by Bill's rubber boots, sleeping on his yellow Helle-Hansen, as they all said hi, shook hands, hugs all around. Sort of like sniffing noses and butts, I thought.

Now and again Bill passed me a french fry or chunk of New York strip steak under the table. Arne's wife, who Arne called White Sugar, got comfortable on Bill's knee. She was about 20 years older than Bill and about 75 pounds heavier. She reached over, and with a loving look at Bill, grabbed his whiskey and tossed it down her capacious fat throat. She liked Bill instantly. She was passionate about him, she was starstruck. But then as I mentioned, women loved Bill, all of them.

She kept her brilliant Russian female wolf-like blue eyes on Arne, and when he wasn't looking she, quick as a white mamba, kissed Bill right on the mouth. I saw her say something in Russian to Bill, then fatly, prettily giggled at her own wit, then she farted. Every one laughed, even Bill laughed, but not with his eyes. He was embarrassed.

From my place under the table by Bill's boots I had one thought and one thought only: this is a bitch in heat. They smell different. You see, we French have a unique understanding and a particular approach to life and sex then most other humans. After all, you humans practice French kissing, tongues in each other's mouths, teeth clashing, and so forth. I never could figure that one out.

White Sugar shared herself, dancing with Smitty, Trig, our engineer, and her husband Arne, but at the end of each drunken rollick out on the dance floor, she somehow always managed to twist herself in such a way to wind up sitting on or by Bill et moi.

You know if you watch wolf bitches in the wild they act a lot like you humans. She managed, somehow secretively, to touch, lick, kiss, and coil around Bill, whimpering.

Bill, somehow, was a primal pheromone for White Sugar. She couldn't keep her hands or lips or whatever off of him. She had gigantic breasts, big as my head which she rubbed Bill with whenever the chance arose, and she found lots of chances. A guy can see a lot from under the table, and I saw a lot. I saw her run her hand up Bill's leg, saw her touch and nuzzle his foot with hers. I also saw Bill, frowning at her, take her hand and move it off of his knee and quietly push it away.

When she dragged him out on the dance floor she was so glued to him that they looked like one large person dancing alone.

When Bill removed White Sugar's hand from his thigh this became red meat for Sugar. She became more aggressive. I've seen this in dogs my whole life as well. Deny the dog a bone and they will kill to get it.

She kicked off her red high heels secretly under the table, one of which landed right by me. I saw this, of course, being under the table myself. With her toes free she moved her foot with her probing toes further up what she thought was Bill's thigh and crotch. She looked at Bill sweetly, encouragingly, as she did her rub. I saw from under the table, however, in her excitement she got off a leg. It wasn't Bills leg and crotch, it was our engineer Trig's leg and crotch.

She was moving her fluttering toes higher and higher and faster and faster. She was sort of grunting. When she rubbed Trig's crotch, massaging with her red painted big toe, he started to get aroused, and groaned a little uff sound. White Sugar, in her drunkenness, thought it was Bill groaning. Then feeling Trig's sexual arousal with her toes, thinking it was Bill groaning, White Sugar rubbed harder and faster. Trig starting to sweat and get more excited. Trig, with his red dot rubber boot started to rub what he thought was White Sugars foot, but was instead Arne's, her husband's foot.

I watch from under the table as Arne grabbed White Sugar's upper thigh. Sugar, thinking it was a new loving gesture by Bill, reached under the table and grabbed Bill's thigh.

Trig, thinking it was me licking his foot, shouted, "God damn it, Frankie," and kicked Sugar in the side of her knee.

She screamed in pain, Trig yelled, Bill stood up, Arne stood up, yelling, "What the hell is going on?"

His wife, the one in heat, grabbed Arne and kissed him on his lips fervently, coiling, laughing, whimpering, and whining. Pretty soon everyone calmed and sat back down.

I watched as White Sugar insistent, stealthily, while laughing and talking to Arne, quietly, so quietly, again reached for Bill's upper thigh and crotch. Her frowning husband saw this this time.

He wagged his index finger in her face, smiling and said, "No no, my little pet."

While Arne was telling White Sugar no no, she got tears in her big blue eyes and pouted sweetly, innocently.

Every one continued to eat and drink, then drink some more. The accordionist droned on. Then in the next instant I felt her reach under the table and grab me by the scruff of my neck, and grabbing Bill's hand she whirled us out onto the crowded dance floor.

The accordionist, downing his sixth Jack, continued up and down the keys of his squeeze box. Changing to Western music he played, "She Got the Goldmine, I Got the Shaft."

Sugar held me close to her body, my head vice-gripped between her cushioning breasts. She held me tightly like this while her probing little chubby white hand hidden beneath my body started to rub Bill.

She got more and more excited, panting even, until in her thrall, she inadvertently dropped me on the floor, her now exposed hand plainly on Bill's crotch and zipper. Her husband saw it all this time, stormed out onto the dance floor, and slapped Sugar and back handed Bill in the same motion.

Smitty threw down a handful of bills on the table and we all were unceremoniously pushed, shoved by the bouncer, and thrown out through the cheap chipped green door into the mist, rain, and distant fog horns. Bill's face was bleeding blood and lipstick.

The next morning when Bill and I awoke the Lynch was settled at a strange angle, bow down. The curtains hung at an odd angle. Rushing out onto the deck, Smitty saw that in his haste to get uptown to drink and carouse and off the boat that in the deep twilight he had placed part of the Lynch's bow under an adjoining dock. When the tide rose, it smashed flat all of our bow rails. No other damage done, except to Smitty's reputation. We took the morning to repair the rails, which took Bill three hours to repair, and we were ready again for wheels up.

Cranking up the cats, we pulled in our lines and backed out into Douglas Channel, Smitty on the watch. Bill held me in his loving arms while we both watched as Ketchikan slid astern out of sight.

Proceeding north, the Cape Fear, throwing a large jade curl off of her steel bow, passed close by us. White Sugar in a red bathrobe swung open the starboard wheelhouse door, springing through it to the railing, waving wildly to Bill. Bill didn't wave back as we watched the Cape Fear pull ahead and away from us into the morning mists as we slogged along, notching a racy waterlogged six knots.

Next, wonder of wonders, the cook finally came out of his stateroom. He had a bottle of Jack in one hand and a cigarette hanging from his mouth. Reaching into the refrigerator he pulled out a meaty beef bone and dropped it on the galley deck for me. Next he made breakfast for the crew, then coughing while smoking his constant cigarette, he leaned out the galley door, spit over the side, then went back into his stateroom, violently slamming his door. Maybe the wind caught it.

The morning was fresh, a rising glass, blue sky as we entered the broad reaches of Clarence Strait northbound. We nosed our way north all day until we reached the the skinniest slot on the inside passage, Wrangle Narrows, between Mitkof Island and Kupreanof Island. We reached this spot in the dark. Coming out at the north end of Wrangle Narrows we passed by Petersburg, Alaska on our starboard, entering into Fredrick Sound as morning was approaching.

Bill and I took the watch just as we were passing the old whaling station Tyee off in the distance to the starboard on the southern toe of Admiralty Island. At this spot we swung northward up Chatham straits toward far off Point Augusta on our distant port side.

Bill's and my watch was up as we approached Point Augusta. Night was falling on a calm sea.

Before tumbling down the stairs to the warmth of our beds, Bill stopped and turned and looked at Smitty, and pointed to the radar. Smitty was nursing a whisky and Coke.

"See out there on our port forward quarter, see that blip? That's a freighter south-bound. Keep and eye out, Skipper. The rain has started again, seems like it always does at dark up here."

Smitty squinted into the rain bejeweled windows.

Bill and I, tired from our watch, climbed into our bunk and soon were fast asleep on the gentle rolling of the sea under misty moon light. The rumbling of the D17000s and the occasional creak of the hull twisting gently in the sea were conducive to sleep.

The sound of the sea gently splashing along the hull was just putting me over the top into dreamland when Smitty screamed down the passageway, "Get out of your bunks and into your life jackets! Oh Jesus, Lord!"

I barked my loudest as Bill leaped from his bunk, running up to the wheelhouse. Bill grabbed the large wooden wheel and spun it hard starboard. In front of us, maybe 150 feet away was the giant, rough, barnacled hull of a huge Russian cannery freighter. The freighter was blowing five short blasts repeatedly. The freighter veered starboard and we veered starboard, thanks to Bill.

Smitty was dazed, even though the crisis was past. He stood frozen, looking into the radar. He smelled of alcohol.

"Smitty!" Bill yelled. "Look at me! We were all nearly killed! Even though you are the skipper and I the mate, there will be no more drinking on the bridge. Smitty, look at me. Did you hear what I said? Go below, Smitty. Frankie and I will stand the rest of your watch. Get off the bridge."

Smitty started to complain, but Bill took him by the arm and forcefully led him to the stairs, leading down to his state room.

Cape Spenser Light came up on our port side where we then entered the highly respected, highly feared great open North Pacific. Luck was with us in that the weather was basically calm all the way from Cape Spenser, across the gulf of Alaska, to Cape Hinchinbrook, the entrance light guarding the rocky entrance into Prince William Sound.

This evening, after a long, boring run from the Yakutat 12 mile buoy, we picked up on our radar Kayak Island, and picked up visually the Cape St. Elias light that was installed on this volcanic remnant in 1916.

The light, with its great Fresnel aero-beacon, is visible 20 miles out to sea. Clear out at sea I could smell the stench of the thousands of walrus living there, along with the massive puffin population flowing like a ritual feathered river around the gigantic cliffs. Pelagic birds, their nesting sites filled with eggs and guano, were everywhere. I could smell them all, but then you know we dogs have a very sharp sense of smell.

Cape Hinchinbrook and the entrance into Prince William Sound and into Cordova came up in the distance just as Bill and I were coming off of our midnight to 6 am watch.

Bill told me that the Hinchinbrook light was visible from 22 miles out to sea and guarded the entrance to Prince William Sound, warning sailors of the dangerous shallows in the area. Bill read every nautical book he could lay his hands on, and told me everything he learned.

Smitty held us to the mid channel as we rounded the southern point of Hinchin-brook Island and headed up Orca Channel to our final destination, Orca Cannery, Cordova.

Bill and I went below and had breakfast. Eggs and bacon and hash browns for Bill, and eggs and bacon and hash browns for me. We sat in the heat of the galley while Bill read navigation and rules of the road. As I snuggled up to him on the galley bench he rubbed my belly, I love that. About two miles out from Orca Cannery we walked out to the bow to wake up and to smell the fresh morning salt-sea breeze. I was excited. For once it was sunny.

As we stood up in the bow, Bill holding onto the railings, we looked down into the rich green waters of Orca Passage. Softly gliding through the mirror calm waters we passed a decapitated salmon head floating with the tide out to sea. We went on toward the cannery.

The closer we got to the cannery the more decapitated heads and tails of salmon there were. Finally we were cutting through a silver sea of heads and tails, all shinning bright silver in the sun light. Each decapitated, bodiless salmon head floating on its side with its one staring eye took on a very spooky look.

The thousands of heads with their one startled eye looking, searching, somehow they all seemed surprised at their decapitation. The overwhelming effect was sudden death. Cutting through this dense sea of silver staring heads and truncated tails, Bill turned, putting his hands over his eyes, and started to cry.

Summer in Cordova was fast paced. We had offloaded our cargo from Seattle, fueled and provisioned up, and were off, out into the Gulf of Alaska to a place called Pete Dahl Flats. Here on Pete Dahl flats and out in the broad and beautiful Prince William sound we were to remain until June-July, taking in fish from the fishing boats during the day and running to offload at Orca cannery at night, the whole thing repeated and repeated. We were all tired, and yet the natural beauty helped.

On our last trip into Cordova, summer fishing season came to a close.

The noble and mighty Copper River kings were on another kind of migration. Plane loads of the ruby red oily kings, sockeyes, and silvers, were rushed south to restaurants and homes where the going price was fifty dollars a pound. The fisherman got a minute fraction of that.

As we left the fishing grounds for the last trip of the season for Cordova, we were all excited to be heading south once more.

Out at the Orca Cannery we loaded thousands of cases of salmon. We also had a full deck loaded with power skiffs, engines and parts, chains and barrels, pallets covered and secure. Anything that could stand the weather and salt spray on our trip going south was lashed on deck, the rest went into the hold.

Our final stop before heading for the open Gulf of Alaska, down the inside, and finally Seattle, was the oil dock in Cordova.

Smitty, the engineer, and the old cook had been drinking all morning, knowing that as soon as we left the oil dock they could take to their bunks while Bill and I would take the first watch.

Coming into the dock, Bill got the bow line fasten on a cleat while Smitty sprung the stern off the bow line into the dock at the stern. The old cook drunk and unstable at best, took the large nylon hawser in his left hand and once again walked off the end of the Lynch, straight into the oily harbor, sinking like a rock. I barked, and seeing what I was barking at, Bill ran back, saw the cook's flailing hand sticking out of the muddy, oiled water. Reaching down, he pulled the old sodden cook over the side onto the deck. He lay there gasping, coughing up sea water and bits of green seaweed. Smitty called 911 and in a moment the old man was off the boat, into an ambulance, and uptown to the hospital.

When Smitty came back on board, Bill said, "Him or me, Smitty."

After an hour or so searching the docks and bars, Smitty returned with a freak show of a man. Purple hair, tattoos everywhere, even on his forehead. He pulled down his lower lip to show Bill and me his social security number, whatever that was. I'm sure dogs don't have social security numbers. He had his tattooed on the inside of his lower lip. His teeth were all rotten and black at the gums. He came on board with a stuffed black garbage bag over his shoulder. He had ragged clothes, smelled like the bars, a cigarette hanging out of his mouth. He was staggering, a Hawaiian carved sharks tooth around his neck on a greasy cord.

Bill walked away shaking his head in disgust.

Fueled and loaded, Smitty yelled, "Cast off."

We backed out into the channel, idle reverse port screw, idle forward starboard screw, turned in our length and headed out Orca Passage to Cape Hinchinbrook on our port into the Gulf of Alaska.

We were loaded to the plimsoll mark and then some. We were riding low in the sea. All of our holds were packed to the top, heavy deck loads lashed, and in some cases covered with canvas. With the Cape Lynch's blunt bow we pretty much stopped at every towering swell, and the swells were huge coming out from the protection of Cape Hinchinbrook into the open gulf. We never took water over the bow, though we slammed every wave with sledge-hammer like force.

Driving through one after another of these massive swells, about an hour out of Prince William Sound we hit one particular high towering wave heavily straight on the bow. We rose high on this titanic wave then the bow dropped like a hammer into the next wave, causing the whole boat to shudder and shake, the twin screws cavitating, causing a hideous rattling death like sound.

Slamming this wave square on shook

the entire Lynch so entirely it broke dishes in the galley, knocked over stools in the wheelhouse, and finally the force of the swell knocked the radar off of its mounts, sending it crashing to the deck, shattering the fragile instrument.

It seemed like the sea in all of its nektonic fury rose up around the Lynch on each titanic swell, holding, engulfing her until the only part of the boat above water as we plunged into each wave was the wheelhouse. All else, the whole boat, was under water.

With all of our weight, a whale of a boat, we all prayed, Smitty shouting, "Come up, come up, God damn it!"

Finally shuttering, stuttering, the twin screws finding green water, she rose into the blanket of blue, her decks gleaming, only to drop again into the towering smooth rolling trough again.

Losing a radar is not insurmountable to

navigating, however it takes a much more intense approach to keeping off the always present stoney islands and rocks that line the inside passage everywhere as well as ships in the night. Your radars are your eyes in all situations, day or night, but especially at night, and fog was always present somewhere.

Running at night without radar requires, demands, close attention to navigational lights at capes, points, and buoys along your route, plus other marine traffic. Then we needed to sync this information with our marine charts of the area. This is called running light to light.

For instance, one starboard cape may flash two short bursts of light and one long, then twelve seconds of quiescence, then the same sequence at this particular light over and over. Seeing this light pattern the person at the wheel checks that sequence with the information on the chart, confirms, and then moves his attention on to the next light. This light may flash three shorts and twelve seconds of quiescence, on the port side, then the same procedure as before, again and again. Check, then coordinate, verify with the chart, then on to the next light, and so forth on down the twisting inside passage to Seattle. Trust the light houses but verify on the chart. Of course out inclosed in giant arm of the Alaskan Gulf there are no lighthouses, no islands only water, lots of it. Out there we run on the clock, our compass, and visual alertness. We were finally on our way south, but first, the gulf.

Luck was with us as this time. Crossing the Gulf of Alaska it was near lake calm except for the long towering swells that never broke, but were as steep as the sides of small buildings. As we approached these swells, Bill pulled back the throttles and we coasted up, then gently over the top, where Bill once more, as the bow softly, hugely, like some rounded stone, dropped, applied both throttles, over and over at each gigantic glassy polished swell.

Half way across Bill said, "What the hell is that floating out there?"

It looked so big and round at a distance until we were along side what turned out to be a large, shell encrusted Japanese glass fishing float with a large Japanese symbol in yellow painted on it. We were in the Japanese current, sweeping west in its polar trajectory arc. Bill told me that some of the only Alaska native masks had bamboo teeth made from drift from the orient. After finding the glass ball there was more of the same towering swells that never broke, extending on and on over the curve of the earth.

Finally, after getting lost in a thick grey early morning fog, we finally broke out, hitting land fall south of Cape Spenser, about 50 miles.

Bill figured out it was Chichagof Island. We turned north, passing Cape Spenser on our port, turning to the starboard, and entered into Cross Sound. Cross Sound marks the northern end of the inside passage down through British Columbia to Seattle. We passed on south, retracing our northern route without incident, passing Ketchikan twinkling in the dark, and out into a glass smooth Dixon entrance, Haida Gwaii Sound and ever south, Seattle our distant goal.

The cook, of course, couldn't cook. Smitty hired him because he could drink and smoke pot, of which he had a large bag. He gave me ice cream off a spoon from the freezer right out of the carton. I ate what everyone else ate, even sitting at the table. I haven't talked much about the cat, but then what dog would? Anyway the cat slept with Smitty and ate at the table with the rest of us. Really he was a pretty cool cat, and one more thing, I never saw a rat or mouse on the Cape Lynch. The only remnant of mice or rats was when we were at the cannery and then occasionally I would find a gall bladder on the deck. That was all, the cat, ate everything else even the fur, yuk!

Queen Charlotte Sound came and went in settled motionless fog and rain.

Finally, after powering south, truly a place of mazes, a place of edge gashing rocky shores, bottom holing passages, we passed Alert Bay on our port side, following a moonlit golden path entering directly into the northern reaches of Johnstone Strait.

Johnstone Strait is a wide and important part of the inside passageway north and south. It is know for its vicious winds, it's confused seas, its rocks and reefs. In other words, a place of seamen's graves and grave danger.

Bill and I had just completed our six hours of watch as we passed Telegraph Harbor Light on the starboard. The weather was fresh, clear, brisk breezes. Stars were gleaming and polished in the crisp deep cold dark violet sky.

Smitty came into the wheelhouse with a Coke and Jack, along with the hippy cook who smelled like pot and held a beer.

Bill looked at this motley crew askance. The iron mike whined on as we frequently changed course directions, heading down tortuous Johnstone Passage, running light to light as we had been since our radar was smashed out in the Gulf of Alaska.

Leaving the wheelhouse, we headed down the passageway into our stateroom where Bill climbed under the grey wool blankets, falling into an instant deep sleep. Navigating takes it out of you.

Bill had been asleep for an hour or so. I was still awake, curled in Bill's strong arms. There was something in me that smelled, sensed danger. That canine sixth sense, you may have heard of it.

The hippy cook from Cordova was playing cards in the galley with Smitty.

I heard them slapping cards on the table, laughing, and shouting, "Fifteen-one, fifteen-two," and a lot of other stuff I didn't know about.

All of their shouts came from the galley. No one was on the bridge at the wheel in the wheelhouse. The boat was on auto-pilot while Smitty and the hippy cook were drunk and stoned.

"That's bullshit," I heard Smitty scream. "I won that hand, you stoned freak." Then they both laughed uproariously, loudly. I heard the galley door to the outside open then close. Then open again, and I heard Smitty laugh and say, "had to drain the main vein."

I now sat up, listening more closely with some fear.

The mumbling, sloppy conversation went on for a while longer when Smitty, slurring his words said, "Hold those cards while I run up and find out where the hell we are." Then I heard him laugh.

I heard Smitty stumble past the door to our stateroom. Then I heard him climb the short ladder to the wheelhouse.

All was quiet for a while, the D17000 cats forcing their huge, power-filled will into the following dark sea, then I heard Smitty yell down to the galley to the hippy cook, "Cookie, get your ass up here a minute."

Since our state room was right next to the wheelhouse, I could hear every word they said.

Smitty said, "What the hell light's that? What was the last light? Shit, that Thai weed you brought really fucked me up. I think that light on the port is Clarence Island, but don't count on it. Could be H'Kusam light as well. Hand me my Jack, Cookie, while I figure this mess out."

"I see a light out there on the starboard. See it, Smitty? Red and green. Maybe that's Clarence light," Cookie said, sounding hopeful.

"Jesus, I guess you are good for something, Cookie. That's a ship heading directly at us."

Smitty, drunk and stoned as he was, turned hard to starboard to avoid the other ship, which shortly passed us on our port. As it passed close by us, it blew five short blasts on it ship's whistle and shined it's search light on us. I heard someone from the other ship shouting at us.

Finally it was quiet for a while, then I heard Smitty say, without conviction, "Ya, I'm pretty damn sure that's Clarence Light. Not positive, but see the light behind it? I think that's Hardwicke Light, and damn it, it should be on the starboard, or is it the other way around it? Cookie, go grab me another Coke and double Jack while I get my brain around this. See there that flashing light coming up on our port? I'm pretty sure that's our turn."

Going past that light about 500 yards Smitty took a hard turn to the starboard. This is what the charts said to do if this was Clarence light.

If this was Clarence light, but it wasn't.

To be off a light in this dark, rock gutted waterway was as close to destruction for a mariner as one could get.

Rules of the road say: if you don't know your position, you turn on your emergency lights and come to a full stop.

Your life hangs on a lighthouse.

There was one significant problem. With all of their attention to their cards, their booze, and pot, Cookie and Smitty had got off a light. This nearly proved to be fatal. To be off a light in this black, stone lined, tortuous passage was tantamount to ending badly.

Running eight knots into soot dense heavy darkness, Smitty and Cookie relaxed, lit another joint, thinking they were finally back on the right course, but they weren't.

Just when the Thai weed was at its strongest, Cookie said, "What the hell is that ahead of us in the water?"

Smitty said, "I don't see nothin' in the water but there, right over where we are a head'n is a mountain, and it's damn close. Holy shit Smitty shouted as he flipped on the deck lights, I see waves on a beach right in front of us."

With that exclamation he turned the Lynch 180 degrees and headed, unbeknownst to him, not slowing, ran straight across Johnstone Strait to the far dark mountainous drift-lined eastern shore.

This route took them perhaps 30 minutes into the dooming dark. Feeling secure they were now on the right course, Smitty sent Cookie below to get some matches to finish their joint and to grab two more Cokes and Jack.

Running at a strong eight knots, feeling good again, they smoked the last half of the joint, finished their Coke and Jacks, just in time for Smitty to yell, "What the hell is that?"

Right in front of the Lynch, clearly lit by the deck lamps, was a foaming rocky hostile shore line, again very up close and personal. Grabbing the wheel, Smitty swung the Lynch completely around another 180 degrees, never slowing down, and in less than 50 yards we ran three-quarters of our length, coming to a jolting, sliding stop on top of a huge flat stone from the shore side after hitting two other rocks getting there. In our dark cold state room I felt us hit the first rocky reef. So did Bill, who was out of his bunk in a moment. I was barking my warning bark, rapidly and loudly.

I felt the Lynch hit the second reef, harder this time. Bill was pulling on his boots. We hit that second reef, and falling against the bulkhead wall swearing, he was out the door and up the stairs to the wheelhouse as we hit the final rock, sliding right up on top it.

Our deck lights were shinning in the dark driven mist. We were high and dry. The engines were still at full power, churning, roiling the shallow water behind us, throwing up sand, seaweed and foam. Running into the wheelhouse, Bill saw Smitty at the chart table, his back to the bow, both engines at full power ahead. The stoned, drunk cook was at the great ship's wheel, trying to steer the grounded boat.

Trigve, the engineer, hastily stuck his head in the wheelhouse door and said there was smoke coming from the engine room.

Bill yelled at Trigve, "idle down the cats!"

Back at the chart table, Smitty said, "Oh

ya, I think I know where we are or should have been." He started to show Bill on the charts where he thought we were. "I zigged here where I should have zagged."

Bill said, "You dumb, dumb bastard. Get out of my way."

We felt the cats slowing and rumbling as Trig shut them down to idle. The Bilge alarm sounded continuously. Finally the auxiliary engine, its tinny sound echoing off of the stones and forest nearby, sounded its strident shrieked, which echoed off of the forest and rocks nearby.

The gigantic stone we had miraculously slid up on was heavily encrusted with green seaweed and bull kelp of all kinds. Crabs were crawling around in the deck lights. There were small fish swimming around in hollowed out pools on top of the rocks. Oil was seeping from somewhere under the Lynch. Smoke was escaping into the night air from the vents. We sat on the rock at a crazy angle, listing the same 12 degrees to the starboard as we were when we disastrously left Seattle, only now we were also down on the stern by about 10 degrees. If the tide rose and we didn't rise with it, the engine room would fill first, and we were then doomed.

Looking out, there were no other lights visible anywhere, just dark. No village lights, no lighthouse lights, no other ship's lights, just ink black. We were at low tide and had no idea if we were holed, and if so, how badly as we were high and dry. The tide would rise, and if we weren't holed too badly we would rise with it. If we were holed badly, we would fill stern first with water and settle to the bottom of Johnstone Strait. If we were gut punched, lost a plank, broke some gaping hole in the bottom, then this could be the ole Cape Lynches final watery grave.

I thought of the old fisherman's warning while standing on the rain dark dock in Friday Harbor. Our bodies, our skulls, would be the playground for the fishes.

As we sat there we were surrounded by a field of glistening, writhing, pulsing, living mass of green. Everything glistened, everything moved, the bottom of the sea exposed to air. We were looking down at the bottom of the sea and it was dry.

Bill grabbed Smitty, drunk Smitty, stoned Smitty, and while looking directly in to his vacuous eyes from five inches away, told him that he, Bill, was going below between the hull and the brine tanks to assess the damage to the hull.

"Listen to me Smitty. Did you hear me?"

Smitty dully nodded.

I could hear the big cats slowly turning over in idle. Bill grab Smitty by his shirt and told him not to try to back off while he was up in the fore hold between decks. If Smitty could back her off with a large hole in her,

Bill would be trapped like a rat in a sewer.

As Bill crawled forward along the port side, he crawled over large oily eight by eight inch yellow cedar cross beams fastened to the oily four by twelve" bottom planks. Crawling closer to the bow, Bill could hear water gushing in. Bill could also see that the powerful pump in the interspace was keeping up with the incoming water. Turning to crawl out of this dark dungeon, he heard Smitty pull the gears into reverse, power the cats back up, and try to pull us off the rock.

Crawling crabbing his way back out of the hold, swearing like the logger he was, Bill came running up to the wheelhouse, grabbed Smitty and yelled into his face, "I should throw you overboard you good for nothing. Get the hell out of the wheelhouse."

Bill got on the phone calling, "Mayday, Mayday. Coast Guard Base Alert Bay, Coast

Guard Base Alert Bay, this is the American fishing vessel Cape Lynch. We have gone aground in the upper reaches of Johnstone Strait. Last recorded light sighting was Telegraph Cove. We are in total darkness outside our vessel. Mayday, Mayday, this is the American fishing vessel, Cape Lynch. We have gone aground in the upper reaches of Johnstone Strait. Last recored light sighting was Telegraph cove. Do you copy?"

"We hear you loud and clear, Cape Lynch," came a clipped Britannic voice. "This is Lieutenant, J.G. Charles Douglas. We will have our search and rescue helicopter in the air momentarily. The crews are powering the chopper up as we speak. Please turn on all of your deck lights."

I thought we were a small mote of light in this vast wilderness. In about 10 minutes, the flashing lights of the helicopter came into sight, flew around us, flashed its lights, and then was gone. We were approached in about two hours by a smallish seagoing tug, the Gikumi, from Telegraph Cove. It stood by and finally, as the tide rose to high, it slowly approached as dawn was also approaching. Attaching to our stern cleats, she slowly, carefully pulled us into deep water as the tide rose.

The Gikumi gave us two friendly blasts on her ship's horn. Bill did the same and once more, port engine in slow reverse, starboard engine in slow forward, Fathometer running, we turned, heading out into flat calm Johnstone Strait. We were holed, leaking about 25 gallons of water per hour, the pumps nicely handling the influx.

Bill sent Smitty and the cook to bed while Trigve, the engineer, made us pancakes, eggs and bacon, and jet black coffee.

Trigve kept his eyes on the pumps as we headed south once more for Puget Sound.

We finally entered the Hiram Chittenden Locks in Seattle, after a day and a half of running slowly this time to help stem the inflow of sea water. Bill had taken some four by fours and a mattress forward to the hole and plugged it as well as he could.

This time as were approaching the old weathered dock there were no riotous drunks on board, no stoned old aunts, no crazy nephews, just sedate motoring at the prescribed speed, dead slow. We were throwing no wake, as motored up to the old West Wall, the place we had left from some months before, Smitty on the bow line, Trigve on the stern line, Bill and me on the wheel. How things had changed.

In those days New England Fish Co. wanted all of the crew off the boat to stop the overtime pay. Given this, Bill packed our gear and we were soon back in Bill's purple Cuda. Smitty, the engineer, and the meth-head cook stayed on the boat to man the pumps and to get the Lynch ready for winter.

Bill and I, flush with cash, headed down to Seattle's Edgewater Hotel, which hung right out over Elliott Bay. Bill said the Beatles stayed there when they were in Seattle. Hum, I thought, ladybugs, stink bugs, why would we stay in a place where there were beetles, insects, maybe spiders? Bill got us a room where, when we opened the window, we looked right down into Puget Sound. We could see fish swimming below in the water.

Bill took a long bath with bubbles and sang songs. I sat on the edge of the tub, admiring my dearest Bill. Was this the same Bill with the chrome 38 Smith and Wesson that tried to kill me? Was he the same man that shot the white wolf on the Yoko? Was he the same man that cried when his mother hit him? Was he the baby, the boy, the young adolescent that withstood such abuse? I see that boy that is now a confident, mature, strong young adult. I didn't need to wonder and worry about him anymore like I once did. As I looked at him, I still saw the boy that time holds for this young adult to use, but he was not a boy. He was the man that remembered the boy, that respected the man, that still remembered the boy. He didn't forget the boy, he didn't forget the man. Is he the same?

Nah, you know the answer, he is a changed man. Give a man or dog some room and watch them blossom. Turn down the screws and watch them wither.

Man must be the captain of his own ship or suffer the consequences.

Climbing out of the tub, he threw on a soft fluffy white bathrobe and grabbed the phone by the bed, and quietly said, "This is Bill Kriedler in room seven. Will you please send up three New York strip steaks, rare, three twice cooked Idaho potatoes with bacon, sour cream, chives on two and hold the chives on the third?" Bill cupped the phone and said to me, "I didn't think you would like chives, Frankie." Back to the phone he said, "A large kale salad with oil and vinegar, a French baguette with lots of butter, also a plate of marrow bones, a small cheese plate, a bowl of beef broth, a couple of lamb chop popsicles, and some French fries. Oh ya, some beef pâté. Also send up a covered dish of vanilla ice cream with a side of crumbled hamburger."

"What?" I heard the person on the other end of the line shout.

Bill quietly said, "Vanilla ice cream with a side of crumbled hamburger, and cream crackers."

Well where do I start? For instance, have you ever had pâté? Must be made in some dog heaven. A plate of bone marrow? God, you must know we dogs will chew all day on a bone just to get a taste of bone marrow by sticking our tongues so far into the end of the bone that our tongues bleed. Ice cream with crumbled hamburger on top, yum and yum. New York strip steaks, a cheese plate? Need I say more? You probably know that we French are great gourmets, but somewhere along the line my dearest Bill learned about international cuisine. I can assure you it wasn't on the Cape Lynch unless it was from some book.

We had a ball. Speaking of which, I do love to chase balls, but I digress. Bill ordered those steaks delivered hot and succulent to our room. He ordered a beer for me and two beers for him.

We jumped up on the king size bed, rough housed a little, then crawled under the covers. I can tell you honestly we ate in bed. What a meal.

We watched a movie while eating in bed about a white whale, Moby something, and after finishing our beers and eating everything else in sight, we both fell into a long deep sleep. It had been a long spring and summer, and we were both exhausted.

We didn't wake up until the next morning when Bill inadvertently kicked one of the plates off onto the floor, waking us. The first thing he did after we both peed, me on a towel, him in the toilet, was he grabbed the phone and said,

"This is Bill Kriedler in room seven. Will you please send us up three New York strip steaks, rare, six eggs over easy, hash browns, black coffee, and a glass of milk?"

Bill showered, then we fished out of our window right from our room. We caught a little bullhead which managed to get thrash and finally wiggle loose when we tried to pull it up, but then no heartburn who

Bill then ordered a croissant and espresso for himself and a vanilla milkshake with bacon bits for me.

Such beauty and such peace as light rain fell outside our window. The islands across Puget Sound sound were distant grey smears. We could see the rain drops making little circles in the still salt water below our window. Occasionally there were the sounds of ship's horns out on the sound, sometimes an ambulance and noises of the city high on the hills behind the water front. As Bill said, " it was so nice to be warm and secure, away from the miserable crew of the Cape Lynch and to be together, just the two of us. Oh yeh, I hardily agreed.

We went up the Space Needle where we had lunch, cod filets and French fries, as the whole restaurant whirled around and around. What a place to eat. This building they call the Space Needle, I didn't know from a hypodermic needle, it is up in space, when we stood on the observation deck we could see the whole city. We saw a baseball game that night. We both had hot dogs. Bill had three, I had one, no bun, Seattle won. After the game we went out and ate in one of the fanciest restaurants that you might ever imagine, a place called the Four Seasons. Think this over, in that restaurant they let me sit at the table, brought me my own bowl of water, and my dinner on a gold rimed Severus plate, lamb with lamb frites, and, of course by now, my favorite, a plate of bones and marrow.

After a long dinner where nearly every waiter came and patted me on the head, they gave me some of the fanciest doggie bones you ever saw to take back to the Edgewater.

"Your dog, Sir," one waiter opined. "What a gargantuan spirit."

One man with a pretty wife who smelled good came up to our table and said, "How much for that dog?" and then he laughed, because he knew the answer. He said, "I can see he is priceless."

"That's right," Bill said. Still he frowned a little at that comment as though I might be for sale.

Bill bought what he said was a Cuban cigar. Standing out on the sidewalk, he took out a shinny little black box with gold writing on it which said, "Four Seasons," opened it, struck a match along its elegant side, the match flared and in that instant I again saw the new Bill. He lit the cigar, then gently smoked it as we walked down along the waterfront to the Edgewater. The cigar smelled like burning fall leaves and high Sierra forest fires to me.

Along the waterfront, Bill took me riding on a Ferris wheel. I had never seen nor been on one of those. Up and up, and down and down, then up and up, then down and down, around and around. I threw up a little.

Two days later we went back to the boat to gather our gear. The old Cape Lynch, our home from Seattle to Alaska for the summer and back to Seattle again, was sunk at the dock in ten feet of water. Water was

over the engines and the batteries everything below the galley deck was submerged
in oily muddy water. Devastation when a
boat sinks and the batteries are covered, for
starters it it fries the electronics.

A man in a nice dark blue suit stood on
the dock looking down at the Lynch. He said
he was from the New England Fish Co., the
owners of the Cape Lynch. He stood sor-
rowfully, sadly looking down at the sunk-
en boat, angry. He looked at us as Bill told
him who we were. Bill asked if he could
help and also could we go aboard and get
our gear which was most likely dry. No he
said about the help, since there was nothing
to do until the insurance adjuster came. He
said yes we could get our gear even though
he should wait for the adjuster, but what
the hell, go ahead.

The man said he had just fired the
whole crew. He said he found them after
storming from one bar to another for sever-

al hours up in Ballard. There he found Smitty and the gang in a bar, drunk as skunks. They had been drinking for two days and nights. The methhead cook was passed out on a bench. Trigve the engineer was slobbering and kissing some poor excuse for a woman, while Capitan Smitty sat hunched over a six ounce glass of Jack.

"The pumps failed, the boat sank, simple as that. No one was at the wheel," the man in the suit said. " This is what happens when people from the company hire friends of theirs who have no merit, experience, judgement or brains for jobs about which they know nothing.

The dark cloud over his face passed and he looked while smiling at Bill and me, and said he had hoped to meet us, as he had heard great things about us.

"You are Bill Kriedler, and that would make your companion Frankie Le Bichon, is that right?"

"Yes, that's right," Bill said.

With this he said he had heard from multiple sources, including Lieutenant J.G. Charles Douglas from the Alert Bay Coast Guard base, what a fine couple of mariners the two of us were.

"He told us of Frankie's frantic barking when you ran aground, and when the old cook fell overboard in Cordova and Ketchikan."

Well it seemed like he knew all about us. Crist Holden was his name, CEO, New England Fish Co. With that he asked Bill if he would be interested in a job with New England Fish Co. next spring.

Bill asked, "What kind of job? I thought we were all fired because the boat sank." Holden said," I know the grounding up in Johnston Straits was not your fault, in fact the Commandant Charles Douglas heaped praise on you for your instant mayday call and the way you performed, getting the

Lynch free.

Mr. Holden then said, "I would like you to take one of our newest tenders next summer to Alaska for New England Fish Co. as captain."

Bill truthfully told him he had very little experience, as he was sure Mr. Holden knew. Mr. Holden told Bill he admired young men like him, with his verve and take control attitude, and that there seemed to be too few young men like him around. He had been in the fishing industry for the last 45 years and had seen the quality of the skippers decline over that period of time.

With that comment, he said, "here is the caveat", he would, with Bill's ok, enroll him into the Coast Guard navigational school this coming fall and winter in Seattle on the company's dime. He said the course would be thorough and rigorous, but that it would set him up with bridge level education where he would be at the hub of running any ship up to 500 tons in any waters. That is he would be taught critical equipment operations, safe navigation, and general watch keeping of the entire crew. He would graduate with a master's degree and would be the final authority on any of the company ships. It was, he said, one of the highest ranks that one can achieve onboard our company vessels. He would shoulder total responsibility and oversee all shipboard operations. Should he desire to move higher into the company's higher echelon, his degree would be a big boost. If someday he were to leave the company, his degree would be valid and travel with him in any outside merchant marine.

Bill said, "You have a deal, but only if Frankie my Bichon can come. He's a water dog, you know."

Crist smiled warmly and said, "I have two Bichon myself. Hell, I might not hire you if Frankie didn't come," and then chuckled warmly. "You probably don't know it, but you two are known up and down the inside passage, news travels fast on the sea. The story about Frankie protecting the old accordion player from that husky in the Cordova House is now legend on the coast. Such courage you have, Frankie. Frankie's barking, which saved the old cook's life when he went over the side, his barking when you went aground, we need people like you and Frankie in our company. You two are the best thing that has happened in this company in a long, long while. I have never felt so good about a hire in a long time.

"One last thing, since I know you have no home here in Seattle, and your old home is sunk there in front of us, you are going to need a place to live."

"Yes," Bill said, "I have been thinking about that."

"Our son, Nevis, just left for Rome to

finish his architectural degree and had been living in our daylight basement. It's now vacant. We have a nice quiet home out in north Ballard looking over Puget Sound and the Olympic Mountains to the west. May Belle, my wife, was saying just this morning over coffee that perhaps we should rent the basement apartment to some nice college person now that Nevis is in Italy. It comes with its own separate private entrance, and even comes with a carport, which is now empty, since Nevis, the owner of a cute little 1962 MkII red MGA, recently had it shipped to Rome. So you will have covered parking for your purple convertible, a big plus in the rainy Pacific Northwest.

"It's a great little apartment. May Belle and I lived in it for a year while we were building the upstairs. It comes with its own kitchen, and it's yours free of charge until you and Frankie leave for Alaska next spring. It's quiet, private, well lit, and will be a great place for you to study. In fact, the office down there served me and Nevis, and now can be yours. It's completely set up.

"It also has a large back yard which Frankie can share with Ottis and Georgia, our two white Bichons."

Bill clutched me so hard I thought I would have to yelp.

He looked Crist in the eye and said through tears, "Yes and yes again. I have never known such kindness in my life except from Frankie." Bill caught a sob. "I will work hard to make you proud, and I will make a positive contribution to the company."

Crist put his arm around Bill's sobbing shoulder and said kindly, "I knew that already, Son, but thanks for saying it. Welcome aboard to my two new captains."

To author and artist Douglas Granum, creation is a way of life.

His inspiration is derived from his travels around the world and an appreciation of the unusual – trekking the jungles of New Guinea, enjoying plein aire painting in northern Urals of Russia, drifting down China's Yangtze River, looking at the stars in a Serengeti night sky, and commercial fishing in the storm-tossed Gulf of Alaska.

As an artist Douglas Granum works with and in various mediums including stone, metal, glass, wood, canvas, bronze and of course, writing. From creation in his studio in Southworth, Washington, his paintings, glass pieces, metal and stone sculptures can be found worldwide.

Find out more at DouglasGranum.com

Other stories by Douglas Granum:

THE GERMAN MUSIC TEACHER'S COTTAGE

WAR NO PEACE

DEATH AND AFTERLIFE ON EL PASEO

ALONE ON THE YELLOW STONE

THE ROSE COVERED COTTAGE

JUDITH'S GAP

Find out more at DouglasGranum.com